FALLING FOR THE GRUMPY GREEK

SUZANNE MERCHANT

ROMANCE

Recycling programs for this product may not exist in your area.

ISBN-13: 978-1-335-47080-5

Falling for the Grumpy Greek

For questions and comments about the quality of this book, please contact us at CustomerService@Harlequin.com.

Harlequin Enterprises ULC
22 Adelaide St. West, 41st Floor
Toronto, Ontario M5H 4E3, Canada
www.Harlequin.com

HarperCollins Publishers
Macken House, 39/40 Mayor Street Upper,
Dublin 1, D01 C9W8, Ireland
www.HarperCollins.com

Printed in U.S.A.

1 2 3 4 5 6 7 8 9 10 HDC 28 27 26 25

A Pact Between Tycoons

Friends by choice... Brothers by law!

Enzo Capelli and Alexandros Galatis have been partners in crime since university, cultivating wild reputations by throwing parties, wreaking havoc and breaking hearts. The one line they vow never to cross? Dating each other's sister!

Enzo is a man of his word. But when Alex's gorgeous sister, Thaleia, asks for his help with a fake dating scheme, he's willing—after all, it's not real. Yet under moonlit Mediterranean skies, their sizzling chemistry soon threatens to consume them both...

Read Enzo's story in

The Trouble with Italian Millionaires by Karin Baine

When tragedy strikes, Alex finds himself father to a little boy he never knew he had. Wholly unprepared for fatherhood, he's in need of a tutor for his son, and when Enzo's sister, Beatrice, arrives on Ithaca to be interviewed, Alex knows she's the only woman for the job—and his heart!

Read Alex's story in

Falling for the Grumpy Greek by Suzanne Merchant

Both available now!

Dear Reader,

How would you feel if your closest friend betrayed you?

As wild, hell-raising young men, best friends Alexandros and Enzo vowed that their sisters, Thaleia and Beatrice, were off-limits, but while Alexandros is struggling to be a father to George, the son he didn't know existed, Enzo has fallen in love with Thaleia and married her.

Isolated on the fabled island of Ithaca, Alexandros is furious and unforgiving.

Beatrice, Enzo's sister, plots revenge on her brother for not inviting her to the wedding. If she can get a job tutoring Alexandros's son and pretend to fall in love with his father, Enzo will be furious.

But before long she realizes that pretense is unnecessary. She is falling for him, for real.

Alexandros once joked that love and commitment were the only two things that scared him, but as the hot summer days pass, he discovers that the joke is on him. The realization that he cannot control his feelings for Beatrice is terrifying.

When Beatrice leaves Ithaca, a piece of her heart is left behind. Will Alexandros dare face his fears to make it whole again?

Suzanne Merchant

Suzanne Merchant was born and raised in South Africa. She and her husband lived and worked in Cape Town, London, Kuwait, Baghdad, Sydney and Dubai before settling in the Sussex countryside. They enjoy visits from their three grown-up children and are kept busy attempting to wrangle two spaniels, a dachshund, a parrot and a large, unruly garden under control.

Books by Suzanne Merchant

Harlequin Romance

Princesses of Palosia

Conveniently Engaged to a Princess

Their Wildest Safari Dream
Off-Limits Fling with the Billionaire
Ballerina and the Greek Billionaire
Heiress's Escape to South Africa
Cinderella's Adventure with the CEO
Best Man's Second Chance

Visit the Author Profile page at Harlequin.com.

For My Family

CHAPTER ONE

BEATRICE CAPELLI STEPPED off the launch and into trouble.

A secret smile tugged at the corners of her mouth, because the trouble was entirely of her own making. So far, her plan had worked seamlessly. All she had to do now was pass the final test and the job would be hers.

She dropped her bag onto the dock, spread her arms wide and spun in a circle, tipping her face up to the flawless blue of the Greek sky. Warm air, fragrant with the scent of rosemary and wild thyme, filled her lungs—a notable contrast to the crisp atmosphere she'd left yesterday, as dawn had tinged the Swiss Alps pink.

Revenge against Enzo, her brother, would be oh-so-sweet. She could imagine his horrified expression when, in a few months' time, she'd break the news that she'd got a job working for his best friend and former partner in the business of breaking hearts, *and* had fallen in love with him. His rage would be incandescent; hopefully even more incandescent than hers had been when he'd told her, without a trace of guilt, that he'd married in secret. She hadn't decided how long she'd wait before confessing that she was kidding about the falling in love bit. A day? A week? Just thinking about it felt delicious.

For fifteen years he'd insisted that his best friend, Alexandros Galatis, descendant of an ancient ruling family of Ithaca, was, like Lord Byron, another former hell-raiser at their Cambridge college, 'mad, bad and dangerous to know'. Especially for innocent girls like his little sister. He'd forbidden Alexandros from going anywhere near her.

When, aged eight, she'd walked unscathed from the wreckage of the Italian cable car accident that had killed their parents, Enzo had become her guardian. It was years before she processed the fact that he'd only been eighteen, and about to start university. He'd always seemed grown up to her. Obsessed with keeping her safe, he'd enrolled her at a strict, girls-only English boarding school.

She'd been bewildered by her survival. It felt as if the universe had bestowed a second chance on her and she'd set about showing her gratitude. She did as Enzo wanted, and was obedient at school. If she was good, she reasoned with herself, she'd prove herself worthy of the stroke of fate that had spared her life, and worthy of the care that Enzo, her only living relative, had shown for her, even though he was sometimes a distant figure.

That hadn't stopped him from marrying without telling her.

Beatrice wasn't sure what had hurt the most. The fact that he'd married in secret, or that he'd married his friend's sister, who, like herself, had been forbidden territory.

Enzo and Alexandros had become friends in their first week at Cambridge University, and they'd agreed that when their sisters grew up they'd be strictly off-limits. During his rare visits to her, Beatrice had listened to the stories of their wild escapades; how they'd been nicknamed Dionysus, for the Greek god of wine and festivity, and Bacchus, for the Roman god of wild celebrations. That was all she needed to know about Alexandros Galatis, her brother said, leaving the rest to her unfettered imagination.

Life at her school had been sheltered and after lights out the dorm had buzzed with whispered conversations. Enzo had chosen Geneva as a safe place for her to continue her studies in modern languages. She'd grown from an awkward schoolgirl into a beautiful young woman, with luminous eyes and chestnut hair, which tumbled in waves down her back, but she'd been unprepared for male attention. Were the quick fumbles and clumsy kisses in dark clubs what the girls in her dorm had giggled about?

Marc had been a little older, with polished manners and an air of self-confidence, and she'd been flattered by his insistent attention. He'd taken her out for sophisticated dinners, and eventually to his bed. She'd let him, because she'd wanted to experience life like everyone else, and he'd filled her wine glass too often. When she cried out that he was hurting her, he hadn't stopped but afterwards told her she'd 'get used to it'. She hadn't wanted to get used to something so painful and unpleasant. Then, he'd accidently let slip that he knew about her background, and her fortune.

When she'd refused to see him again he'd branded her as cold, and moved on.

It was then that the realisation hit her that not everyone liked her for herself. For some, her fortune and social status as a member of one of the richest families in Europe made her a desirable, perhaps useful friend. The knowledge had confused and hurt her. How would she ever know if friendship was genuine or self-serving? So when she began her teaching career at an international Swiss school, she shortened her name to Bea and adopted her middle name as her surname.

There was absolutely no way Alexandros Galatis would know she was Enzo's sister.

She'd seen pictures of Alexandros and swooned over how much he resembled her imagined idea of Dionysus, a youthful, beautiful man with long hair.

She was about to meet him in person for the first time, and she couldn't wait.

After a night in Athens and an early flight, she'd anticipated taking a taxi to the port and the ferry across to Ithaca. Instead, she'd been met at Kefalonia airport by a liveried driver holding a sign which bore her name. He'd whisked her out to a waiting car, taken care of her luggage, and driven her to the harbour, where this launch—the *Penelope*—had gleamed at the quayside, all white paint, stainless steel trim and varnished deck, her engine a low, throbbing beat on the morning air.

Once clear of the harbour, the engine had roared to life, the kick of speed pressing Bea back into the deep cushions of her seat, and the bow wave curling away in a creamy arc as they'd roared towards Ithaca, Kefalonia's smaller neighbour.

Enough surprises for one morning, Bea thought, as she bent to pick up her tote bag, swinging it over her shoulder and turning towards the hills that climbed out of the sea. Holm oaks and pines clothed the slopes, and between their dusty green branches she glimpsed the faded pink walls of a Venetian façade, a pillared portico, wooden shutters painted dark green at the many windows and the rusty-red clay of a tiled roof.

Iannis, the middle-aged man who'd piloted the launch, hoisted her bag into the back of an open-topped Jeep, which stood in the shade of an overgrown oleander, and invited her to climb into the passenger seat. Sending a spray of pebbles and sand into the air, he swung the vehicle in a tight circle and onto a track that climbed upwards, between the trees, and then swept around a circular driveway, stopping in a cloud of dust in front of the palatial mansion she'd seen from below.

Quiet descended like a blanket as Iannis cut the engine. Lilting birdsong and the cool trickle of water from a stone fountain were the only sounds Bea could hear, as she sat, suspended between her sheltered, predictable life, and the self-imposed challenge, which lay ahead of her. Doubt and anxiety suddenly made her tummy swoop and she shivered, despite the heat.

But it was too late for regrets.

Iannis strode around the bonnet of the Jeep and opened her door. She released her grip on the safety bar, straightened her spine and sucked in a deep breath. Then she slid out, smoothing down her calf-length linen skirt and adjusting the collar of her blouse. Heat prickled beneath the heavy knot of hair at the back of her neck and gravel crunched beneath her practical sandals. Faced with the grandeur of the mansion in front of her, she felt stupidly pleased that she'd painted her toenails in a shade of shimmering pink. She hoped that defiant little touch of glamour would not detract too much from the image of eminently suitable tutor she wanted to project.

The double doors in the shadow of the portico

creaked open and Bea readied herself to make the best possible impression on the man with whom she intended to pretend to fall in love.

But it wasn't Alexandros Galatis who stepped across the threshold. Bea's startled gaze met the dark eyes of a whip-thin older woman. Her greying hair was pulled back into a severe bun, her mouth a strict line in her olive-skinned face. She glanced downwards and spoke in Greek.

Bea's eyes followed hers, and her heart clenched.

Bright blue eyes fringed with impossibly long, dark lashes gazed up at her. The little boy had a mop of honey blond curls, pink cheeks and an expression as solemn as a baby owl. He wore a white collared shirt tucked into grey shorts, white socks and buckled leather shoes. Hardly, Bea thought, comfortable clothing for a Greek summer's day.

'Welcome,' the woman said, in careful English, extending a hand, 'I am Dafni.' Her handshake was firm and brief. 'And this is George.' She tapped his shoulder.

George stepped forward and thrust a hand towards Bea. He chewed on his bottom lip for a moment and then she saw his chest rise as he took a deep breath.

'I am pleased to meet you, Miss Bea. Will you teach me…English?'

Bea dropped into a crouch in front of him, bringing her eyes level with his, and took his small hand in hers. His eyes, surely the colour of a summer sky, held a mix of shyness and hope.

'I'm pleased to meet you, too, George, and I would like that very much.' The conversational Greek she'd picked up from past pupils wouldn't take her very far, but she saw the surprise on Dafni's face at her use of the language.

George's forehead creased in concentration and then he nodded. 'Thank you. *Efharisto.*' Bea suspected he'd used up his store of English, and that he'd been thoroughly rehearsed in delivering his greeting. 'Very much,' he added, after a pause.

Bea followed them into the entrance hall and up a curved staircase which swept to a gallery where the walls were hung with oil paintings. The décor spoke effortlessly of generations of wealth. Plush velvets layered with brocades, in jewel colours, added luxury. Eastern rugs were scattered on the ancient floorboards, which gleamed with the patina of centuries of footfalls.

Her accommodation on the first floor was a suite consisting of a traditionally furnished sitting room and bedroom but with a bathroom that gleamed with modern brass fittings and cool white marble.

George, who had been silent since his stilted greeting, was a world away from the confident children she taught. They were mostly boisterous, often getting into mischief, accustomed to travelling and mixing with multicultural families. Her heart, already captured by this little boy, ached at the thought of his isolated existence on Ithaca.

As he and Dafni withdrew he turned to look back at Bea over his shoulder, his blue eyes fixed on her face.

Was this love at first sight?

In his study at the Villa Eirini, Alexandros Galatis heard the growl of the Jeep as Iannis changed down a gear to negotiate the steep slope, before swinging onto the driveway and cutting the engine.

He stood and strode to the tall windows. The view of dark green trees, sparkling sea and cloudless sky stretched all the way to Kefalonia, and could be distracting, even to his fierce ability to concentrate, but today his interest was focussed on something much closer.

The woman he hoped would be George's tutor had arrived. From his vantage point on the first floor he could look straight down onto the driveway.

Although Iannis had opened the passenger door and was busy lifting a bag from the back of the vehicle, the woman—who from where he stood looked no more than a girl—sat unmoving in her seat, her hands gripping the bar on the dashboard, her head a little bent.

Her slender neck was mostly obscured by the glossy knot of chestnut hair, which rested at her nape. As he watched, she released her grip on the bar, raised her head and dropped her shoulders. He caught a glimpse of sandaled feet, a mid-calf skirt and demure blouse as she slid to the ground. The elegant leather bag, which she pulled over her shoulder, looked slightly at odds with her general air of modesty.

He hoped, very much, that Bea Antonini was going to solve some of his problems. Teaching George to speak English was the first one. His son, now four, needed more than the dependable and traditional Dafni could give him. She spoke little English, and Alex was determined to honour the boy's English mother by ensuring he at least spoke her language fluently. God knew, he'd done nothing else for her, although he would have, had he known…

Guilt slammed into him. However familiar the emotion was, and two years had been long enough for it to become his close companion, it showed no sign of relenting. Not yet. Would it, ever? He pushed a hand through his hair and rolled his shoulders, trying to release the tension he held there, 24-7. Unanswerable questions lined up again to taunt him.

Did George look like his mother? Alex had the vaguest, fleeting memory of the woman who'd been just one of many one-night stands at that time of his life. Blonde, blue eyes, lithe—that was about as far as it went. What would he tell the boy when he was older and started asking questions about his mother? That he hadn't known of his existence until after she'd died? That he'd never given her another thought, after he'd walked out of her apartment in the early hours of the morning, until that day he'd received an email informing him he was the father and only relative of a two-year-old boy? That he would have helped her if he'd known she was pregnant with his baby?

He liked to think he would have done the right thing. But he suspected the only support he would have provided would have been financial. He'd been too busy making an excess of money by day and spending it by night to be bothered to do anything else.

Dragging his thoughts back to the present, he watched the new arrival disappear into the Villa Eirini. The house had been built on the site of an older dwelling by his great-grandfather. The name meant *House of Peace* and Alex smiled grimly at the irony of it. Since he'd brought George here, his own personal peace had been in short supply.

Quiet and isolation were almost a given. But peace—what did that even feel like? He was conflicted, guilt-ridden, confused. George had become the most important thing in his universe, but he still needed to run his multibillion-dollar property development company, travel to sites and resorts across the world.

Delegation was not his strong point. His father had denied him control of all aspects of his life and then shipped him off to university in England, but gaining his freedom had not meant he'd taken control of it. Instead, he'd created havoc, living on the edge, indulging in his passions for danger, speed and women. Discovering he was a father had hit him and his lifestyle like a wrecking ball. Two years on he was still trying to recover. He'd tasted excess, and stratospheric success, but being handed responsibility for his two-year-old son terrified him. What if he found he was unable to care for him properly?

There were no guarantees in life. It felt to Alex as if he clung to safety by the finest thread. What if that snapped and George came to harm? Sometimes he woke at night, in a cold sweat, worrying about it.

He wouldn't have believed that a two-year-old could turn his life upside down, or that the first time he heard him mutter 'Dada' against his shoulder, he would have felt a rush of emotion so powerful it had stolen his breath.

It had stolen his capacity for rational thought, too, and caused him to take his attention off his sister. One day she was launching a business, and the next, it seemed, she was emailing him—*emailing*—to tell him she'd married his best friend.

He wanted to punch something. Okay, *someone*, and that someone was Enzo, the best friend in question. They'd sworn, practically on their lives, that their sisters were both much too good and innocent for the likes of them. Had all those years of friendship been meaningless? They'd trusted each other, without question. Well, *he* had, anyway. Thaleia and Enzo had taken advantage of his distraction with George. They'd married behind his back, without telling another soul.

He uncurled his fists and tried to breathe through the feeling of betrayal.

He felt marooned in a sea of indecision and pressure, pulled in every direction but unable to decide which one to take.

He needed someone who would care for George assiduously so he could get his life back on track. He did not want to be caught out and knocked sideways, ever again.

Dafni was doing an excellent job, but George needed to experience more, learn more. From the beginning he'd spoken to him in English as well as Greek, but they lived on a small Greek island, surrounded by Greek staff…

Was the girl who must be, at this moment, meeting his son, going to be able to fulfil the strict requirements of the task?

The testimonial from the school where she taught was glowing. She seemed to be the perfect fit for the job, but would George warm to her? That was the most important requirement of all.

Alex glanced at his watch. He'd instructed

Dafni to show Miss Antonini to her suite and then asked for coffee to be served in the courtyard half an hour later.

He was a good judge of character. He'd know in minutes if she was suitable.

Or not.

CHAPTER TWO

'MISS ANTONINI?'

Bea twisted round in her chair. The voice was deep, dark and grave and the perfect match for the tall, broad man crossing the shaded courtyard towards her. There was no trace of lightness in his expression.

He wore dark trousers, a pale blue business shirt and navy silk tie.

Seriously? In Greece, in June?

He stopped two paces away, his big shadow darkening the white tablecloth. 'I apologise for keeping you waiting.' He pocketed a pair of chunky cufflinks and began to roll back the cuffs of his shirt, each fold revealing more of his tanned, corded forearms. Then, as if he'd read her mind, he hooked an index finger into the knot of the tie, pulled it loose and undid the two top buttons of his shirt. 'I was on a business video call. Hence…' He gestured to the tie that now hung loosely around his neck. He extended a hand.

Dear God, he was hot—devastatingly handsome—and her mind leapt to an X-rated zone, which, until now, had existed hidden inside her head. Could the simple act of undoing a tie and buttons be sensuous?

Trying to gather her wits, while aware that she was making the worst first impression ever, Bea scrambled to her feet. The chair snagged on a table leg and in her hurry and confusion, it tipped over, landing behind her with a crash.

Alexandros Galatis ignored it. His steady gaze was trained on her, taking in her blouse and skirt, sandals, *painted toenails*. Probably, he found her wanting on every single level and she hadn't even opened her mouth yet.

His eyes moved back up to her face. What had he asked her? Ah, yes. Her name.

'I… Yes.'

His handshake was firm, his palm dry. The greeting lasted mere seconds, but it was long enough for Bea to feel a tremor run from his hand into hers, and up her arm, all the way to her heart. Startled, her eyes flew to his, but his appraising look was unruffled. There was no sign he'd felt it, too.

She dropped her eyes, her heart racing, her breath shortening. She had to gain control of this situation, even if to hear with dignity that he found her wholly unsuitable for the job of tutor to his four-year-old son.

Among her young pupils at the school in Geneva were the sons and daughters of royalty, diplomats and statesmen. She and her brother had been left rich beyond many peoples' imaginations. Meeting this Greek tycoon should be easy. Except, her fevered mind insisted, none of the one percent of the richest and most privileged members of society had ever caused her brain to go into meltdown or her body to respond to their handshake as if she'd been plugged into a live socket. She resisted putting a hand up to her hair to see if it was standing on end. Every inch of her felt hypersensitive to him.

He inclined his head, and his eyes flicked to the chair, which lay upended, its legs in the air, behind her.

Bea turned and bent to right it, but Alexandros was there first. His hand brushed across her fingers as they each took hold of the same forest-green metal leg, and the buzz of sensation confirmed that the effect of his handshake had not been a one-off, never-to-be-repeated event.

'Allow me,' he murmured, as he set the chair on its legs and made a movement with a hand. 'Please, Miss Antonini, sit down.'

Bea sat, stiff and upright, and folded her hands in her lap. This meeting was not going the way she'd anticipated. Nothing felt certain, except the fact that her plan had already failed on two counts. She hadn't allowed for the rush of emotion she would feel towards George, or the full meltdown she'd experience under the measured, dark gaze of his father.

Perhaps all she could hope to salvage from this wreck of an interview would be her dignity, even if she had to gather up the shreds of it from where it lay about her. She drew in a breath, trusting that her pumping heartbeat was not visible through the cotton of her blouse, and raised her eyes.

Alexandros pulled out the chair opposite her. At some point during her confusion, a tray of china cups, a cafetière of coffee along with a jug of milk and a silver bowl of sugar had been brought to the table.

'Coffee? With milk?'

'Yes, please.'

The hand that gripped the handle of the glass jug was strong and its only adornment was a gold signet ring on the little finger. The ring looked old—perhaps centuries old—with a soft patina and a barely-discernible design of what could be a family crest.

She placed the porcelain cup and saucer in front of her, relieved when they didn't rattle.

Alexandros Galatis leaned forward in his chair, raised his cup to his mouth and studied her over the rim. The cup looked tiny in his big hand, but his hold on it was light.

'Tell me, Miss Antonini, why you think you are the right person to tutor my son?'

Bea blinked. This was a waste of time. She'd

already demonstrated, in the space of a few minutes, that she was nervous, clumsy and incoherent. After all, employers routinely made up their minds in the first five seconds of a meeting whether or not they would hire the candidate and then used the rest of the time to prove to themselves that their initial instinct had been correct.

Here they were, already deep into the proving stage.

Since her fate had undoubtedly been sealed, his decision made, there was nothing she could do to redeem herself. Shock at her reaction to him robbed her of concentration and focus. It was outside her experience and she had no idea how to deal with it. The confidence with which she'd stepped off the launch, not an hour ago, had vanished. Her plan to work for Alexandros Galatis, to annoy her brother, felt childish and shallow now, in this atmosphere of gravity, in front of this forceful, burdened, dark man.

He seemed to be a different person from the close friend Enzo had described, although she imagined *that* friendship, since Enzo had married his sister, now only existed in some part of the planet that was perpetually wrapped in the permafrost.

She searched her memory for anything her brother had told her about George or his mother.

It had been a one-night stand, and the news that he was a father, and that the child's mother had died had been a seismic shock to Alex and his friends and family. Was he grieving a woman whom he scarcely remembered?

And George? The look of cautious hope in his eyes had wrenched her heart. How could she use a bereaved little boy to implement her plan to take revenge? It felt manipulative and selfish now she'd met him. What had she been thinking? Her cheeks heated with shame. She bit her bottom lip and squeezed her interlaced fingers together.

'Miss Antonini?'

'I…whoever you appoint…would need to be sensitive to George's unique…situation.' She hesitated, searching for the right words. 'He…how long has he been with you, at the Villa Eirini?'

He placed his cup on its saucer and his hand curled into a fist. The fingers of his other hand raked through the thick waves of his hair, leaving it messy. Close up, she could see fine threads of silver at his temples, and a thin, pale scar sliced across the left side of his forehead.

She remembered the story of how he and Enzo had partied late one night and been locked out of their college. When he'd tried to scale the wall Alexandros had fallen. Then her brother had frowned. Alexandros's father, he'd said, had been more concerned about his son possibly being thrown out than the fact that he was in hospital with concussion and six stitches in his head.

'George has been here two years and two

months, almost to the day.' Alexandros flexed his fingers, keeping his eyes on her face. 'I was… unaware…of his existence until shortly before that.'

'His mother died in an accident, didn't she?'

He tipped his head to one side. 'How do you know that?'

'I… Your PA told me, in one of the interviews.'

'A speeding car failed to stop at a pedestrian crossing. George's pushchair was flung through the air and even though he was securely strapped in, he was knocked unconscious. But…it could have been him who…' His voice cracked a little, before he took a deep breath, sighing it out. 'I… don't like to think about that.'

'No.' Bea curbed a strong and unwise impulse to reach out a hand to him, to offer comfort. If she massaged those tense shoulders would the hard muscles soften and relax? She waited a few moments for her heart to resume its normal beat before asking quietly, 'And his mother?'

He pressed the tip of an index finger against the bridge of his nose and closed his eyes for a beat. 'She died instantly. One minute she was pushing George across the street in his pushchair, the next he was without a mother and had become my responsibility. I'd had absolutely no experience with children, and…I'd planned to keep it that way. He's had to deal with huge trauma and change. Strangers telling him they're his grandparents, learning to accept me as his father. A different language. When it happened, I believe he was speaking as well as any two-year-old, but he's hardly spoken since. That's where you come in. Could you help him?'

Stress radiated from the deepening lines between his eyebrows, the rolling of his shoulders and the way he leaned towards her, his dark olive eyes fixed on her face. The photographs Enzo had taken of his friend had shown a man with a shoulder-length mane of thick, dark hair, and eyes that glinted with intentional trouble and a wicked sense of fun. The man who sat opposite her bore little resemblance to his younger self. He looked world-weary, anxious and as if his patience was on a timer. If she failed his scrutiny, if she didn't tick all the boxes he had lined up in his head, she had no doubt he'd tell her why, immediately.

Unwittingly, her own eyes dropped to his mouth. The surprisingly sensuous curve of it was compressed into a severe line. Distracted, she wondered if he ever smiled. What a waste of that mouth if he didn't. *Could she make him?*

Mentally, she'd already talked herself out of the job and so he'd asked her a question to which she had no honest answer, but she'd have to try to find one.

'I have a three-month summer break, which I want to use productively. Teaching George feels like a worthwhile way to spend the time.'

That was honest, at least. In the few minutes she'd spent with George he had captured her heart. She would love to teach him—teaching gave her pleasure and satisfaction—but more than that, she'd like to inject some fun into his life. This beautiful house felt like a museum, where everyone tiptoed through the rooms in reverential silence. She wondered if the walls of this courtyard ever echoed to the sound of George's laughter, or the flagstones to the patter of his feet.

'And you would want to return to Switzerland at the end of the summer? In September?'

She nodded. 'I thought that was acceptable, from the wording of the advertisement.'

'Yes, but an extension could be considered, under the right circumstances. Although life here is quiet and it can feel isolated.' He frowned. 'Especially for a young woman.'

'Oh. I…don't mind that, but I hadn't considered the possibility of staying on after the summer.' If she brushed the pad of her thumb over his forehead, would those lines fade away and his real face—the one she'd secretly fantasised over in Enzo's photographs—reappear?

'So you regard this as a summer job. But there's not much nightlife on Ithaca. At least, not around here.'

'Bars and clubs aren't my thing. With its history, beautiful landscapes, the sea and beaches,

I'm sure Ithaca has a lot more to offer than a hangover.'

Interest sharpened his expression. His eyes widened.

'Would you expect to teach George some of that history? Take him for walks? Go swimming?'

'Naturally. Learning is about much more than sitting at a desk and reciting the alphabet...'

'George,' he cut in, 'has a strict timetable. Dafni finds it easier if it is not disrupted.'

Bea thought of Dafni's severe hairstyle, her straight mouth. She was sure she was kind, but she was also sure she was no fun, at all.

'Children learn more easily and certainly more quickly if lessons are made fun.'

'Fun?'

'Yes.' She was on a roll and, after all, there was nothing, absolutely nothing, left to lose. 'Fun and playtime are essential. Strict timetables, for a four-year-old boy, are begging to be disrupted. They're frustrating and limiting. If I feel depressed by the thought of a strict timetable, and I do, you can be as sure as Penelope was faithful to Odysseus...'

'Was she?'

'Of course she was.'

'You'd tell the story to George?'

'I would. But as I was saying, you can be sure that if I find a strict timetable depressing, George must find it unbearable. At his age, boys are far less able to sit still and concentrate than girls. It's been proven.'

If he'd had any doubts about his decision, she'd just obliterated them. She'd be on the *Penelope* back to Kefalonia this very afternoon. There might be a flight to Geneva this evening, if she could get back to Athens in time.

'So. Learning about the history of Ithaca. Trips to the beach. Swimming.' He nodded. 'That all sounds like the summer job you have planned for yourself. School was never fun in my day.'

That, thought Bea, was glaringly obvious. It was hard to believe that this man had been the friend with whom her brother had raised hell at university, almost been sent down, and gone on to make an obscene amount of money while living a life that involved a lot of work, and a lot—a *lot*—of play. Perhaps he'd used up his allotted amount of fun.

That didn't mean his little boy shouldn't have some, but she wasn't going to be the person to help him find it.

She felt the heat of his gaze land on her again. She remembered the way her skin prickled at the feel of his hand enclosing hers, the way that bolt of something had sizzled and scorched its way to her heart, and then onwards, downwards…

Leaving would be the sensible, safe and honest thing to do. Another tutor could be found for George, and he'd soon forget her fleeting visit.

She'd thought this would be easy, but she'd only been thinking of herself and her need to get back at her brother.

It wouldn't be easy at all. How could it be, when Alexandros made her feel as if he saw right into her head, read her frankly unacceptable thoughts. She would be his son's teacher, in a position of trust. Wondering how it would feel to have those strong fingers stroke her cheek, his thumb brush her lips, his arms wrap around her…she'd already had all those thoughts, and she couldn't unthink them.

All she could do was…regret she'd ever come to Ithaca. Her brother had been right, for all those years. She didn't need to know his friend. He may not be mad, or bad, but…*dangerous*? He was lethal.

Her self-made trouble suddenly felt reckless, deep and very scary.

CHAPTER THREE

ALEXANDROS GALATIS SAT back in his chair. He'd drunk half of his cup of coffee and the remainder of it had grown cold. He didn't care.

Cups of coffee could be replenished. Listening to this young woman expound her theories on education was much more interesting.

Her ideas were far removed from the regime he and Dafni had devised for George, but he was prepared to admit that he was probably out of touch. His own schooling in Athens had veered between crushing boredom and creative threats. Boredom at the dry, dull teaching of subjects that held little interest for him, and threats from his father about what would happen if he didn't try harder and do better.

Listening to Bea upended all his ideas. He'd employed Dafni because she'd reminded him of his own childhood nanny, who'd been strict but kind and stood out in his memory as someone who had shown him affection when there'd never been any demonstration of love between, or from, his parents.

Surely George needed structure and routine, after the trauma he'd been through. After all, he himself found comfort in orderliness. He hated surprises. He didn't like the sudden realisation that his attempts to become a good father were failing because in trying to impose order on what had become his own disorderly life, he was unwittingly recreating the conditions of his own unhappy, emotionally sterile childhood.

He was already getting this completely wrong because he was ignorant of how a healthy relationship between a father and son should look. His father had demanded perfection, and he had never been able to achieve anything near it. He'd never been good enough, but as a child and teenager he hadn't possessed the emotional tools to recognize the futility of striving for perfection.

Was he setting George on a path towards the same distant and unloving relationship he had with his own father, simply because he knew nothing else? Even worse, was he becoming *like* him? The idea chilled him. He wanted his son to be happy, to feel valued and loved, but he'd handed over much of his care and education to Dafni, while he tried to get some sort of normality back into his life, resuming his punishing routine of travel and work. Dafni, although kind, was not equipped to give George what he now realised he needed.

It was not surprising that when he'd escaped, to England and Cambridge, he'd erupted like a genie who'd been trapped in a lamp for ten thousand years, determined to live life to its fullest and most precarious potential. And, on day one, he'd found a friend to take along for the ride.

His right hand clenched. They'd been best friends, bolstering each other through the bad times and celebrating the good times together. Jokingly at first, but later in earnest, they'd vowed to protect their little sisters from each other.

Bea Antonini's eyes followed the movement, and two faint, questioning lines appeared between her eyebrows.

Something about her stirred a deep-buried memory. He frowned and folded his arms across his chest, tipping his head back to glance at the sky before returning his eyes to her face. It wasn't anything as obvious as her eyes, although they were memorable. Wide-spaced, grey and fringed with long, dark lashes. In certain lights, he thought, they might be green.

And it wasn't the smooth sweep of her chestnut hair, twisted into a knot at her nape. He wondered how long it was when she unpinned it.

Not as if that was relevant. Her appearance was of no consequence. Her ability to help George was what mattered, and that was what he *should* be considering.

Perhaps it was his lack of female company, over the past two years, which made the arrival of a beautiful intelligent young woman at the Villa Eirini so arresting. So…unsettling.

Because her tamed hairstyle and modest clothes couldn't hide the fact that she *was* arresting. And beautiful. He blinked and studied her again.

It was something to do with the tilt of her chin and the directness of her no-nonsense gaze that made him think he'd seen her before, but that was impossible. According to her CV, she'd been incarcerated at an English girls' boarding school from the age of eight, despite her Italian heritage.

Her parents must have been keen for her to learn English; just as he was, for George. And her English was faultless, her experience perfect for the role of tutor.

'You say, on your application, that you're fluent in…four languages?'

Bea Antonini raised her chin, a little, and returned his gaze. 'Yes. English, Italian, French and German. I studied modern languages in Geneva. I also speak a little Greek.'

He inclined his head. 'Where did you learn that?'

'I taught two Greek siblings. I picked it up from them.'

Impressive. 'Does the school where you teach…'

He pushed his fingers through his hair, aware that the reflexive gesture was something he did too often. He'd allowed his hair to grow longer from the day he left school, and when he'd first reverted to this more conservative style he'd missed it, but he was used to its shorter length now. 'Does it follow the principles that you've described? Does the curriculum include…*fun*?'

'The school believes in a rounded education for all its pupils. That includes outdoor activities as well as learning in the classroom. Fresh air and sunshine, in summer and winter, are a given. No child is expected to sit at a desk for long periods. They're encouraged to participate, question and make mistakes.'

'*Mistakes?*' He couldn't disguise his surprise. 'I thought mistakes were usually—*always*—punished.'

'Making mistakes helps children to learn. If a child is terrified of getting something wrong, they'll be afraid to try. They need to test boundaries, and themselves. George comes across as being afraid of saying the wrong thing, so he says nothing…'

Constructive criticism was a good thing, he told himself, smothering a cryptic response. But criticism of George was a different matter. She'd barely met his son. She knew very little about him.

'George is not…' he began, but then he stopped. If there was one quality he valued above all others, it was honesty. That, and directness, were the pillars that supported his business and personal beliefs. It was the reason he had accepted responsibility for George. It had been shocking and bewildering and he'd had to make huge changes to his lifestyle, but once the DNA test had proved he was the boy's father it had never occurred to him to duck responsibility for him.

He was renowned in the business world for being fair and straight-talking. His fortune had been made honestly. It might have been harder that way, but for him his principles were non-negotiable.

It was obvious that Bea Antonini was honest. She might want this job, but she was not going to compromise herself to get it, and he admired that.

'I apologise. I wasn't criticising your son, rather the teaching methods…' She smiled, and Alexandros felt as if the sun had found its way into the shady courtyard and bathed it in a warm glow. 'He's a beautiful little boy and I'd love…' After a beat of silence he prompted her.

'You'd love…?'

'I was going to say I'd love to get to know him better, but it's obvious that I'm not the right fit for this position.'

He narrowed his eyes. There was a small pulse beating, way too quickly, at her throat and the way she'd gripped her hands together in her lap had turned her knuckles white. Was she obscuring something? Did she really want this position, and feared she'd blown her chance of getting it?

Could she be hiding behind her demure clothes and hairstyle? The women he knew liked to show off their beauty. They flaunted their bodies, in tight-fitting tops and short skirts, let gorgeous, lustrous hair like hers flow freely. The only hint of glamour about her was the shimmery pink polish on her toenails and that looked out of place with her low-heeled, sensible sandals. Beneath her blouse and skirt, was there a luscious, curvy figure? Creamy skin? He imagined pulling the pins from her hair and feeling it slide through his hands like rich satin. If he rubbed a thumb across her full bottom lip, would her eyes flutter closed, her breath stutter…

Alexandros slapped his thoughts away. God, as soon as he'd solved this issue of George's tutor, he'd get himself away from Ithaca for a few days, to somewhere he could be anonymous, and find some female company, at least for a night.

He should be over one-night stands. He should have focused on finding someone to settle down with, who might be a mother to George. But the idea of a ready-made family sent most women running in the opposite direction, and when the hell did he have time to form a lasting relationship with anyone?

Not that he planned on ever finding a forever partner for himself, he simply wanted stability for his son. His parents' marriage was a perpetual argument. He sometimes wondered how they'd stopped fighting long enough to have him and his sister. If that was wedded bliss, he'd decided, years ago, it was not for him.

What if you married someone, had a kid and then the relationship turned toxic?

Never.

'Is that what you think? That you're not the right fit? You're certainly honest, Miss Antonini.' He kept his eyes averted from the tender-looking skin in the dipped neck of her blouse. He hadn't made up his mind about her, yet, and he didn't want to give her the wrong idea. He may well decide to send her away and look for someone more suitable…more *conventional.* 'And I value honesty highly.'

She pulled that lush bottom lip between her teeth and nodded, without raising her eyes. He needed to end this conversation and get back to his study, where he could block out thoughts of how this woman made him feel. Business plans and financial forecasts worked almost as well as a cold shower.

But although he knew there'd be a hundred emails waiting for him, and probably as many missed messages and calls on his phone, he wanted to prolong this meeting. The courtyard was cool and calm, protected from the fierce heat of the Greek midday sun and any outside activity that could intrude on his thoughts. He could work late into the night to compensate for time lost during the day.

He wanted to probe a little deeper into Miss Antonini's personality; find out what made her tick, and what didn't. When last had he had the opportunity to sit opposite a beautiful woman and have a proper conversation with her, with no time restriction.

He couldn't remember. His encounters with women were short, sometimes sweet and always, absolutely always, forgettable. He'd made sure they understood, from the beginning, that there'd be no long, lazy morning after, no second date and no exchange of phone numbers. The sort of women who were comfortable with his terms were the kind whose agendas generally matched his own.

Since George, there'd been no women at all.

He pulled in a deep breath. Whatever he thought of her, and however much he wanted to continue sitting here, enjoying her company, this had to stop. He stood, stretching out a hand, at the same time acknowledging to himself that touching her was a very bad idea. Perhaps he'd need that cold shower, after all.

She stood, too, and her hand barely brushed against his before she withdrew it.

'I'll just…thank you, Mr Galatis. I haven't unpacked, so…'

'George,' he said on impulse, 'will be having his lunch in the schoolroom. Why don't you join him? See how you get on?'

She shook her head. 'Would that be wise, since it seems I'm not the person you're looking for? If I gave a misleading impression in my application, and the video calls with your PA, I apologise.'

'I think it's important for George to meet his possible tutor in a relaxed setting. And if this doesn't work out…what was that you said about learning from mistakes?'

Lunch with George was bittersweet. She watched him eat his meal, nodding or shaking his head in response to questions from Dafni, chewing his food carefully and picking up his plastic tumbler of water with both hands, not spilling a drop.

She tried to think of a way to elicit a response from him. His watchful eyes stayed on her as she walked around the schoolroom, examining the books on the shelf and the neat stacks of writing and drawing paper and pots of pencils. Finally, she picked up two books and sat down again at the table.

'Which of these books do you like best, George?' George pointed at the book in her right hand. 'Ah.' Bea turned the book over. 'Can you tell me why?'

He studied her for what felt like minutes and then spoke softly.

'He says because it is blue,' Dafni translated back to her.

Bea wanted to high-five someone, but Dafni was an unlikely participant in what she saw as her small triumph in getting a response from George. Her heart ached for him, in this structured universe, which had been created with the best of intentions, but which felt stifling and unnatural.

She wondered if he had any memories of his mother, and how growing up without her would affect him. She remembered the sense of bewilderment and confusion at the shocking and sudden change in her life when she and Enzo had been orphaned.

At her boarding school, each Sunday, she was required to write a letter home. While the other girls wrote to their parents or grandparents, Beatrice wrote to Enzo, telling him of her successes and failures, of friendships and feuds. She rarely heard from him but looked forward to his occasional visits when he'd paint a picture of the colourful life he seemed to lead. She'd longed to finish school so she could embark on an exciting life of her own, when he might admire her achievements and admit her to his circle of glamorous friends. She wanted him to be the affectionate, teasing big brother she remembered from her childhood, before everything changed.

She'd never imagined he would marry someone—*anyone*—without telling her. She was his only family, as he was hers. Surely families stuck together, especially ones as small as theirs. She'd felt crushed and curiously belittled when he'd told her, as if she counted for nothing by the person from whom she'd most wanted recognition. Her belief that she mattered to him was shattered and when the sting of hurt had subsided, anger had replaced it. She'd determined to show him he no longer controlled her.

Dafni informed her that after his lunch George spent quiet time with a book. There were sandwiches in the kitchen for the staff, she said, if Bea wanted anything to eat. While Dafni supervised George's meals and all other aspects of his day, a younger member of staff helped him to dress in the mornings and gave him his bath in the evenings.

Bea paused in the doorway, watching George choose a book, acknowledging a tug of regret that she'd never see him again, but she knew that was the very best that could happen. Even if, by some miracle, she was offered the job, she'd leave again within three months. George needed someone who would dedicate themselves to his education for the long term, to grow his confidence and prepare him for the day when he'd have to go to school.

Now Bea sat in the velvet-covered armchair at the open window of her sitting room. An afternoon breeze ruffled the surface of the sea, sending white-capped waves dancing across it. Closer, the wind soughed through the trees that covered the slope down to the curve of the shore. In the distance, Kefalonia had shaken off its morning shimmer and settled into a solid shape of hills and valleys, beaches and coves.

She could see Iannis on the *Penelope*, at the jetty, no doubt preparing to take her to Kefalonia, and safely away from Alexandros. The way she'd reacted to him had been mind-blowing. Her body had not felt like her own, responding to his touch, his voice, the watchfulness of his olive-green dark eyes feeling like a caress one minute, and the next as if he was seeing through all her protective layers, right to her soul.

That wasn't the way she'd planned for things to go. In her imagination, she'd had this situation firmly under her own control. She'd do the job and then gleefully inform her brother that she'd been working for his former best friend and had, surprise-surprise, fallen for him.

But she couldn't stay. Not with the way Alexandros made her…*feel.* Unstable, breathless, shaky—she could go on. And on. He undermined her confidence, just by keeping those dark, steady eyes on her face. He made her want to feel her hand in his, again, but at the same time the thought terrified her because she didn't know what to do with her response.

She'd thought she could control this situation,

and the knowledge that she couldn't was frightening. Control meant safety and maybe she'd lost sight of that in her anger with Enzo. These feelings were not what she'd intended to happen and panic fluttered in her chest. If she was going to fall for someone, it had to be on her terms, in the security of her own environment. It would have to be for someone she trusted, whom she knew would value her for *herself.* If Alexandros found out who she was…she felt hot with shame. She'd lied to him, and allowed him to think she was honest.

The only safe thing she could do was leave.

CHAPTER FOUR

THERE WAS A soft tap on the door. Expecting a member of staff coming to tell her she'd be leaving as soon as possible, Bea stood up, cast one last glance at the mesmerising view and turned away from the window.

'Come in.' Her throat felt constricted.

But the person who walked in was Alexandros Galatis.

He'd kept his sleeves rolled up and the tie that had hung loosely around his neck had vanished. As he stopped in the middle of the room he folded his arms over his chest.

The gesture made him look broader, bigger. It pulled the fine cotton of his shirt across his shoulders and above the open second button she could see a dark dusting of hair.

Bea swallowed, her mouth dry. How could she ever have been so naive as to believe she'd be able to do this? Alexandros Galatis's reputation was no secret. She'd sat, wide-eyed, as a girl, listening to the stories of the trouble he'd orchestrated with

Enzo as his wingman. There was no shortage of beautiful, glamorous women swooning over his fallen angel looks, willing to put aside their principles in exchange for a brief spell basking in the heat of his attention, or to experience his legendary skill as a lover.

Or there hadn't been until he'd discovered he had a son. Once the intense public interest in the case had waned, he'd disappeared. The pictures of him, with his mane of unruly hair, direct stare and mouth slightly tipped up at one corner as if at a secret joke, had vanished from the gossipy glossy magazines and from social media. Enzo said he'd retreated to Ithaca to raise the boy, then he'd brushed any further questions aside. His unwillingness to talk about him made sense when she discovered he'd married Thaleia.

Forewarned by her knowledge of what he was like, why had she believed she could withstand the sheer impact of his looks and his personality? Just because he'd given up the bad-boy lifestyle didn't mean he'd fundamentally changed.

She'd kicked off her sandals when she'd returned to her suite and now she stood in front of him, barefoot, feeling like a schoolgirl about to receive a reprimand from the headmaster.

Irritated at being caught off guard, she straightened her spine and raised her head.

'I wasn't expecting you…'

His gaze roved over her, examining her in detail, as if he needed to convince himself that she really was the person he thought she was. The knowledge that she wasn't made her cheeks flush.

Her bag stood near the door and he glanced at it.

'You haven't unpacked?'

Bea shook her head. 'No. Fortunately not.'

'*Fortunately?*' His brows drew together. 'Why?'

'Because it seemed like a waste of time seeing as I assumed you'd be asking me to leave.'

His frown cleared, and he nodded, once. 'Ah. I see.' He rolled his shoulders and pushed his hands into his pockets. His eyes left her face and moved to the window. 'Is that what you want? To leave?'

'I…yes.' There was no point in pretending otherwise. 'Since you don't see me as a suitable tutor for your son, I think it would be best.'

He walked past her and then turned, his back to the bright afternoon light.

'I went to see George after he'd finished his lunch.'

She nodded. 'Before his quiet time with his blue book.'

'His *blue* book?' He tipped his head. 'I'm not sure I understand?'

Bea bit her lip, wishing she hadn't said anything. His bass voice, with a hint of roughness, hit her somewhere below her breastbone and sent tremors radiating along her limbs, making them feel unreliable and unstable. And also not fully in control of the words that came out of her mouth.

He raised an eyebrow.

'Oh…yes.' She considered what she should say. 'I asked George why he preferred a particular book and he said it was because it was blue.'

'He spoke to you?'

'He responded to my question. I was pleased… I didn't try to make sense of why he liked the blue book. I was just glad to get a response…'

'Mm.' He nodded slightly. 'When I asked him if he'd enjoyed his lunch he said yes, because you were there.'

'He said that?' Bea couldn't help her smile of pleasure. 'I'm glad he didn't mind my questions.'

'He also asked if you are going to be his teacher. I'd like to offer you the job.'

Bea stared at him. Then she shook her head. 'Everything you've told me about how you expect him to be taught goes against the methods I use. I don't see how…'

He held up a hand and she caught the gleam of his signet ring. 'Yes, you would represent a big change for him. But he likes you, and for me that's the most important factor.'

Bea pulled her eyes away from his and looked down at her feet. Her pink-tipped toes curled into the soft rug beneath them. 'I'm…very pleased that George likes me. Of course I am, but…'

'It's been…difficult…to know whether he is genuinely happy or merely trying to please. His happiness and well-being are of the utmost importance to me.' He stopped and Bea raised her eyes. She saw his chest rise and he dragged a hand over his face. 'What happened was unimaginably traumatic. I have to do the best I can for him and I owe it to his mother that he learns English. It's the one way I can think of honouring her. That, and making him happy.'

'Naturally, as his father, you want the best for him. But surely you need to find someone more permanent. If he becomes attached to me it'll be another loss when I leave.'

'We'll deal with that problem when it arises. There'd be an opportunity to extend your contract.'

'I must tell you now that I would not consider that option. My life is in Switzerland.'

'I respect your honesty, and your directness, but please consider my offer. I guarantee not to interfere with your teaching or expect you to change your approach in any way.' He turned towards the window, the light showing up the faint lines of stress and fatigue around his eyes. 'At least stay until tomorrow.' He lifted his shoulders and Bea saw again the rigid tension he held there. 'If you'll have dinner with me this evening, we can talk through this.'

'I…don't know. Maybe that's not a good idea…'

How could she tell him that agreeing to dinner felt reckless and dangerous? As if consenting would be like letting go of a rope that served as her only lifeline. If she cast herself adrift, ignoring the warning bells clanging in her head, she didn't think she'd be able to save herself.

'Please.' His voice was low.

Bea's pulse rocketed and a tremor of panic made her shiver. That one word hit home and made her doubt all her reasoning and determination.

And suddenly she knew what she had to do. If she refused the job he'd try to persuade her to change her mind. He was, she remembered, known for almost always getting what he wanted. He would expect her to capitulate, like everyone else in his life.

Alexandros Galatis valued honesty and integrity above all else and so she would be honest with him. She'd tell him the truth: that her brother had married his sister without telling her, and it had hurt her more than she thought possible. That she'd applied for the job of tutor to George, fully aware that it would infuriate her brother. That she'd… No. She wouldn't tell him the bit about pretending to fall in love with him. He didn't need to know that.

Once he knew who she was he'd want her off the island. He certainly wouldn't want her going anywhere near his son again. He believed her to be honest and she'd duped him. He'd be furious with her and angry with himself.

He walked to the door and turned back to look at her, his long fingers curved around the antique brass doorhandle.

'Dinner at seven, on the terrace?'

Bea nodded. 'Thank you.'

'It's rare…very rare…for George to express a liking for someone, or even something.'

The door clicked shut behind him.

Alexandros dropped the report his PA had prepared on Bea Antonini onto his desk, clasped his hands behind his head and looked up at the ancient painted ceiling.

Why had she changed her mind about wanting the job?

He thought over their meeting again. There'd been a spark of something between them. Recognition? He would never have forgotten meeting her, and her name was unfamiliar. Attraction? That was undeniable. He'd registered it from across the courtyard, the moment their eyes had made contact. And then when he'd taken her hand in his—he breathed in, controlling the jolt of his response to the memory, but reliving the warmth that had travelled from her palm to his, up his arm, giving him the irrational feeling that he wanted to keep holding on to her, to keep the connection intact.

It had felt like an anchor, holding him in one place, after two years of being tossed from one problem to another, unable to find a fixed point of safety from which he'd be able to reshape his life.

Just as George had seemed to be finally settling and beginning to speak, allowing Alex to think that life might shake down into an admittedly new normal, his sister had married his best friend. Anger and guilt had warred in his soul, taking it in turns to torment him. He'd felt betrayed by the sibling he'd looked out for, fought for when his father had wanted to refuse her the opportunity of further education, and protected, as much as he could, from the dangers and difficulties of the world. Evidently, he'd failed spectacularly.

Thaleia hadn't made it easy, breaking her heart over someone who jilted her at the altar, but eventually she'd settled down and flung her energy into launching a silver jewellery business.

He'd thought she was past doing anything reckless or outrageous.

How wrong had he been? While he'd retreated to Ithaca to try to protect his son, his best friend had become distant, his sister unreachable. Only when he'd received that email from Thaleia, telling him they were *married*, did he realise why they'd both become evasive.

The betrayal had been double—his sister, and his friend. He and Enzo had sworn their sisters, when they grew up, would be off-limits. At the time the idea of their little sisters ever growing up and having *boyfriends* had seemed ludicrous. They'd laughed at the idea, but sworn anyway. His friend had broken the pact and Alex doubted the anger he felt would ever subside or the trust be rebuilt. Even more difficult to deal with was the fear he felt for his sister's future happiness.

It was possible that nobody knew Enzo as well as he did, and that's what made him afraid. With their dark good looks and the easy charm that came with wealth, they'd cut a swathe through a bevy of beautiful, desirable women. He'd made it clear, to whoever necessary, that relationships and commitment were strictly off the cards. He'd seen enough of his parents' brittle marriage and the fractured relationships of friends, to know that love was something invented by the manufacturers of diamond rings and soppy Valentine's Day cards, to trap the unwary.

But Enzo had had no such scruples. He'd broken more than a few promises and left shattered hearts in his wake. There was no reason at all to believe he'd changed his ways and the thought that he might treat his sister with his usual carelessness made Alex ball his hands into fists. Had the way he'd warned her off Enzo made her fall for his charm and the promise of a lifestyle steeped in luxury? Growing up, they'd been starved of affection and attention. Perhaps it wasn't surprising that Enzo had been able to convince Thaleia she'd find all the love she craved with him.

It wouldn't have happened if he'd kept a closer watch on his sister and now he'd have to shoulder the added burden of anxiety about her future happiness.

Today he thought he'd finally found someone who would take away some of the worry about George that he, as an unprepared father, carried. George liked Bea and he felt instinctively that the little boy would respond well to her.

He liked Bea, too, perhaps more than he should.

He had to come up with an argument that would make her stay.

Persuading women to do his bidding had never been a problem. He'd hardly ever—okay, *never*—had to work hard at it.

But something about Bea's direct gaze and straightforward attitude made him think she wouldn't fall for his charm or looks or be fooled by his focused attention.

And he was two years out of practice. All his persuasive powers over the past two years had been expended on convincing George that he was safe and loved and that his father was not going to disappear in a few seconds of mayhem, crossing a quiet London street.

What would he do if Bea was as determined to refuse his job offer as he was to change her mind? What if he ran out of ideas?

What if he'd lost his touch?

CHAPTER FIVE

THE STONE-FLAGGED TERRACE lay at the back of the mansion and was accessed from a drawing room through tall glass doors. The hallmarks of timeless grandeur, reserved good taste and generations of custodians were evident everywhere. Mirrors, some mottled with age, reflected ruby velvet upholstery, pale silk cushions and intricate Persian rugs. Twin chandeliers, unlit in the dusky light, hung from a plaster-moulded ceiling. The window drapes were held back by loops of thick silken ropes, a flourish of tassels weighting their ends.

Bea stopped inside the door, looking around, taking in the oil portraits, the fine porcelain lamps with linen shades and the collection of silver in a glass-fronted cupboard beside the carved marble fireplace.

The idea of a fire in the grate in June was unthinkable, but she had no doubt that in January winter could make Ithaca a bleak place, and this mansion, warm and welcoming in summer, might feel cold and isolated.

Her feet sank into the thick carpet, muffling her footsteps as she crossed the floor.

Alexandros stood at the edge of the terrace with his back turned towards her, his wide shoulders stiff. He'd changed into black jeans, which rode low on his hips, and a cream linen shirt with the sleeves rolled up to the elbows. As she watched, he pushed a hand through his hair and then dragged it across the back of his neck.

Her green silk dress made her feel good. The swish of the fabric around her ankles was soft, the straps narrow. It gave her confidence, which she knew she needed. The soles of her sparkly sandals clicked on the glazed terracotta tiles, and he turned.

Surprise flashed across his features, but then unmistakable relief softened the stress lines of his forehead and he took a step towards her.

'You're here.'

'Yes. I am.'

'Thank you.' His voice was quiet, his gaze darkly compelling in the fading light. He held out a hand, indicating a circular table covered in a white cloth. Fat candles in dimpled glass globes cast a flickering light over porcelain, silverware and crystal. 'Please, do sit down. May I pour you some wine? White, red or rosé?'

'Oh…white, please.'

His understated manners were smooth and quietly confident. He took her pashmina from her arm and dropped it over the back of the chair she'd chosen, then drew a bottle, frosted with condensation, from a silver bucket and poured wine into glasses. Then he raised his, tipping it towards her.

'Thank you, again, for coming.'

Bea matched his gesture. 'Thank you.'

The intensity of his attention made her feel that she was the most important person in the world to him at that moment. If she knew nothing of his background and reputation it would be easy to fall under the spell of his formidable charm. But she suspected he had a flipside, which was just as forceful, judging by his meteoric rise into the realms of the super wealthy.

She wouldn't want to get on the wrong side of him, but that was exactly what she was about to do.

A young woman appeared at her side, offering warm pitta bread and rich olive oil. It was a long time since she'd had a sandwich in the kitchen after George ate his lunch. She felt hungry, but her mouth was dry. Her head was filled with what she needed to say to Alexandros, and her heart bumped against her ribs when she thought of how angry he'd be. And he'd be perfectly justified.

'Are you comfortable in your suite? If there's anything you need, please let me know.'

'I...yes, thank you. It's a privilege to be in such a beautiful and historic home. Have you always lived here?' Bea smoothed the silk of her dress over her knees.

'No.' Alexandros shook his head and glanced up at the façade of the old building. The last of the sunset was dying in the west, casting a magenta glow across the sky and tinting the faded walls of the house a deeper shade of pink. 'My great-grandparents built the Villa Eirini on the site of an older dwelling.' He lifted his glass to take a mouthful of wine. 'My family is one of the oldest on Ithaca.'

Bea watched the smooth skin of his throat move as he swallowed and she gripped the delicate stem of her wine glass a little too tightly.

'Yes. The Galatis family has been here for centuries.'

His dark brows drew together. 'You know that?'

It was Bea's turn to swallow. She didn't want to give anything away to him before it was necessary, but his nearness fractured her concentration, sending her thoughts along forbidden paths.

'I…did some research.' She smiled and dropped her gaze. 'What would we do without Google?'

'Mm.'

Plates of tender lamb skewers on a bed of spiced rice with a tomato and feta salad arrived at the table. Bea savoured the delicious aroma, hoping that her hunger would defeat the nervous clench of her stomach.

'Did you often visit, when you were a child?'

He nodded, watching her take a mouthful. 'I came here to my grandparents for many holidays. Later, when my sister was old enough, we were sent here with our nanny. Our parents have always preferred the bright lights and restaurants of Athens. They were happy to stay away.' He lifted the bottle from the wine bucket and topped up Bea's glass. 'After my grandparents died the house was locked up for years. My parents wanted to sell it, but it had been bequeathed to me. My grandparents knew how much I loved spending time here, and that I'd cherish it. Then, when… George came, I decided to bring him here. It's safe, and healthy, away from the pollution and noise of a big city. I needed somewhere for him to heal. I had to do some renovations. Updating of the bathrooms and kitchen. Redecorating most of the rooms.'

'It's truly beautiful. Has living here helped George, do you think?'

He lifted his shoulders and frowned. 'To an extent. Yes. I've tried to build a routine for him, so that he always knows what to expect. No shocks or surprises. I have no idea of what his life with his mother was like. But he still hardly speaks. I…don't think I'm getting it right.'

Bea was reluctant to learn any more about George. The memories of his bright, solemn eyes and his earnest manner were already going to stay with her long after she left Ithaca. The more she knew about him, the more difficult he would be to leave. She tried to take a deep breath into lungs that felt constricted by sudden emotion. 'There is something I need to say to you…'

But he interrupted her.

'I saw George again, this evening. I always say goodnight to him, if I'm here.'

'Oh. Do you read him a bedtime story?'

'I… No. Dafni does that, after I've been in to say goodnight.'

'Perhaps you could read to him sometimes. He'd know then that he had your undivided attention. That sort of time spent together is very precious. And very valuable in building lasting bonds and memories.'

'Do you speak from personal experience?'

'I lost my parents in an accident, too. My memories of my mother or father reading to me are some of the most precious ones I have of them.' Bea hesitated. 'What else do you do with George, apart from saying goodnight to him?'

His brows pulled together and he shook his head a little. 'After his quiet time in the afternoons, his *messimeri*, Dafni brings him to my study if I'm not travelling. I ask him about his day. Sometimes we go for a walk in the gardens and sometimes we bring his crayons and paper to a table out here, because he seems to like drawing.'

'Do you enjoy your time with him?'

Bea could sense his frustration. 'I would…if

I knew he was enjoying spending time with me. It's difficult to know, when he expresses so little.' He shook his head. 'I'm often interrupted. My phone…' He shrugged. 'Being available twenty-four seven has its drawbacks.'

His study of her face was questioning, and he frowned, again. 'You make me think of… no matter. What I wanted to say is that when I said goodnight to George this evening, he did say something. He asked again if you are going to be his teacher. I told him you were still deciding, and I'd know tomorrow.' He sat back in his chair, his eyes still on her face and Bea felt that he could read every emotion that crossed it. 'So, my question, Miss Antonini, is this. What answer will I give him in the morning?'

Bea nipped at her lip. She took a deep breath and placed her knife and fork neatly on her half-empty plate. The food had been delicious but now it tasted like sawdust.

'I haven't been honest with you, and I want—I *need*—to put it right.'

'How?' He shook his head slightly. 'You've been completely open and honest about what you see as reasons not to accept this position. They can be overcome. I don't see—'

'What you have failed to see, because I have hidden it, is my true identity. Or my motives for applying for this job.'

He leaned forwards, his knuckles a bone-white

grip on the edge of the table. 'Your *identity*?' His voice dropped, barely audible. 'Who are you, if you're not who you say you are? Are you a journalist? From one of the tabloids? Because if you *are*…'

Bea's heart hammered so loudly that she was sure he would hear it. It made her breathless and a little light-headed. 'No, I really *am* a teacher. All that is true. But my real name is…is not Bea Antonini.'

His eyes narrowed, glittering in the candlelight, and the generous curve of his mouth flattened into a thin line. 'Then who the hell are you?'

'I—I'm Beatrice Capelli. Enzo is my brother.'

There was a beat of stillness before Alexandros surged to his feet in one swift movement, leaning towards her. A glass tipped over, spraying water across the table. It splashed onto Bea's chest and dripped into her lap. He ignored it, his knuckles pressed to the tabletop, his eyes boring into hers. Lines of anger and shock etched his handsome face.

'What?'

The word reverberated in the silence. Bea wondered if the staff had heard his raised voice, or the crash of the glass, and would come out to investigate. Bending her head, she stood up, mopping at her dress with the thick linen napkin that had been spread across her lap.

'I'll go back to my room,' she said, her voice

shaking. 'And tomorrow I'll take the ferry back to Kefalonia, if you will call a taxi to drive me to the port.'

The rasp of his indrawn breath was rough and incongruous on the gentle evening air. Corded muscles threaded his forearms, every line of his hard body drawn tight. He shook his head.

'No.'

'You don't want me here. I completely understand that.'

'Whereas I understand nothing at all. And until you've explained yourself, you're going nowhere.' He straightened up, slowly, never taking his eyes from her face. 'I suggest you sit down again and start talking. I have all night to listen.'

Bea felt behind her for the seat of the chair and lowered herself onto its edge. She curled her fingers around the metal armrests. Opposite her, Alexandros had resumed his seat, too. He leaned back and folded his arms across his chest, but the way his fingers gripped his biceps gave away how tightly he was having to hold on to his temper. Briefly, his eyes left her face. They dipped down to her chest for a moment, then flicked back up.

Bea longed to spread the linen napkin, even though it was damp, over herself. The silk of her dress was delicate and thin. She cringed inwardly, imagining what it must now be revealing in its soaked state. But she fought against feeling intimidated. She didn't look down. There was no point in having her fears confirmed. If she knew her underwear was showing through her dress, it would simply make her feel more exposed and vulnerable.

She could explain everything—well, almost everything—to him. He could be as angry as he liked. She was prepared for that. But apart from wasting his time, which she understood was precious, she hadn't done any real harm. Apart, a voice whispered to her, from raising hope in the heart of a confused little boy and then dashing it again.

But she was coming clean. Being honest. That was what Alexandros wanted.

She bit down on her bottom lip. What she couldn't be truthful about was the way he made her feel. How his brief touch had electrified her, and how she felt a connection to him that felt dangerous, and if she didn't break it, she'd be hurt, because sooner or later *he* would rip it apart.

'I think,' he said evenly, 'you should tell me what the sister of my former best friend, now my *brother-in-law*, is doing here, with a fake identity.'

Bea increased her grip on the chair and used it to keep her spine stiff and straight. 'It's because he's your brother-in-law that I'm here.'

His dark brows rose. 'Sorry, but you'll need to do better than that.'

'Yes. I know.' She nodded. 'You were—*are*—angry about their marriage?'

The sound of the hiss of his breath chilled her in the warm night air. She released her fingers from the chair and reached behind her, pulling her pashmina around her shoulders and clutching it across the wet fabric of her dress.

'He—*your brother*—was my closest friend. We had a pact, about our sisters. We made it on the day after we met. He broke it.' He tipped his head back. 'You ask if I'm angry about their marriage? I came here to Ithaca, to this house, the one place I've always felt safe and…*valued*, to try to protect my son, to help him through his trauma.' His eyes bored into hers again. 'They thought—*they knew*—I was distracted. That I wouldn't know they'd even met, let alone grown close. So yes, I was—I am—furious, about their marriage. But more than that, I feel betrayed, by my friend and by the sister I've protected all her life.' He shook his head, his jaw working. 'But I don't understand how that brings us to—*this*.' He reached for his wine glass and swallowed a mouthful, his throat jerking.

'I was furious, too. They didn't tell me about the wedding, either, until afterwards.' The remembered hurt welled up inside her, again.

He shifted forwards, propping his folded arms on the table. 'Enzo and I agreed that love, outside the realm of friendship, is a dangerous idea. It can be used as manipulation. It can turn to dust. The example of my parents' "love" put me off from a young age. If love can make a man's closest, most trusted friend betray him, it's even more treacherous than I believed.'

'Their excuse was that they wanted a quiet wedding. So quiet that nobody knew about it.' Bea could hear the bitterness in her own voice. 'When our parents died, so suddenly, I was eight. The cable car we were travelling in crashed to the ground, high in the Italian Alps. My brother is ten years older than me, and he became my guardian. I know now that he was terrified of something happening to me. The day of the accident, he'd taken the same cable car up the mountain earlier and skied down. He'd had to wait for hours to discover who had survived, and those hours of uncertainty scarred him. He was terrified by the fickle nature of fate and he became obsessive about my safety.' She lifted her shoulders and dropped them again. 'My survival was so random. I was shocked but unhurt. Our parents, and others, died. Enzo began to see danger and catastrophe around every corner. He'd experienced how suddenly life, and love with it, could be snatched away. He never let me meet you, his best friend, because he said you were dangerous, especially around innocent girls like me, and sisters were off-limits. He told me about the pact you'd made. So…'

'So he betrayed you, too. I get that you're angry,

but not—' he gestured towards her '—why you're here.'

'This was supposed to be *my* revenge. I wanted to work for you, get to know you, and—' she hesitated '—and then tell him afterwards, because I knew he'd be furious. He'd always made sure I was kept away from you. He's tried to control everything I've done, but mostly from a distance. He chose Geneva for me, because he decided Switzerland was a safe place for an innocent eighteen-year-old to study. I had to fight him to persuade him that I wanted to teach. Our parents left us wealthy, and I don't need to work, but I wanted to do something meaningful with my life, especially for children.' She took a deep, shuddering breath. 'I'd been so lucky, and I needed to give something back. But mostly I wanted to show him that I no longer need him.' Her voice caught and she swallowed. 'Like he obviously doesn't need me.'

To her dismay, Bea felt the hot sting of tears behind her eyes. She would *not* cry in front of him. She pressed her lips together and clenched her teeth so that her jaw ached.

A measure of understanding softened his features. 'What made you decide to tell me?' He sounded genuinely puzzled. 'I might never have known.'

'It was when you said how much you value honesty and integrity. Both are qualities I've always tried to cultivate. I found I didn't want to live a lie, especially where the feelings of a small boy were at stake, no matter how much I wanted revenge on my brother. Faced with everything George has had to deal with, at such a young, impressionable age, my motives felt petty and manipulative. His well-being is the most important thing to consider. I didn't want to be the sort of person who lost sight of that, to satisfy, or justify, my own need to pay my brother back.'

This was all true, but the fact that she was lying by omission was a bitter irony. The real reason behind her determination to get away was Alexandros himself.

He nodded. 'I would agree, but I do wonder about your motives. Are you expecting me to feel sorry for you? To ignore your attempt to deceive me so you can bask in the righteousness of your confession? Because, despite your last-minute attempt at soul-saving honesty, I need you to leave Ithaca as soon as possible. Trust was another necessary attribute, which I possibly failed to mention. Your brother was the only person I thought I could trust, completely, and now I've discovered how wrong I was. Consequently, I'd never be able to trust you and I cannot countenance the idea of you having anything, at all, to do with George.'

'No, I don't expect sympathy, I don't need it. I just wanted to explain why I had resisted becoming George's tutor after I had the chance to meet him.'

* * *

Alexandros watched Beatrice walk away.

Her head was high, her back straight and her shoulders squared beneath the creamy pashmina she'd wrapped around herself. The silk dress hugged her swaying hips and its flippy hem brushed against her ankles. She looked composed and unhurried, and it made him angrier.

How could she be so calm when he could barely contain his fury, at her for attempting to deceive him, and at Enzo and Thaleia for… For what? For keeping him out of the loop? For falling in love, when they'd agreed that love was a figment of an overheated imagination that would last no longer than a morning mist?

Or simply for hurting him, by being more important to each other than he was to them?

They'd hurt Bea, too, and although he didn't understand why, that made his own hurt worse.

Now Bea—*Beatrice*—had tried to use him as a way of getting back at her brother.

He pushed his chair roughly away from the table and stood up, the thought of sitting out here, on this beautiful evening now intolerable. He'd been convinced he'd be able to persuade her to stay.

As she'd turned to leave, she'd expressed regret, for trying to deceive him and for wasting his time. What if he'd swallowed his pride and accepted her apology? Would she have stayed?

He thrust that thought aside before it was even fully formed.

At least, though, he'd been right about something. The feeling that he'd seen her before, or somehow knew her, had been justified. He had an encyclopedic memory for faces and now the picture Enzo had kept on his desk, of his kid sister, grey eyes smiling into the camera, clicked into place in his brain. She must have been about ten, then.

Enzo had told him about the accident in which they'd lost their parents, but had subsequently never wanted to talk about it. And Alex, as an eighteen-year-old student, tasting sweet freedom from his restrictive home and school for the first time, hadn't been empathetic. Now he wondered at the depth of trauma his friend had suffered and how he'd kept it hidden, along with the fear that he might lose his sister, who'd survived by some random stroke of fate, too.

Had Enzo's wild lifestyle been a result of that trauma? Perhaps he'd constantly needed to taunt fate to see how far he could push it.

He strode into the drawing room, where he poured two fingers of single malt into a glass, and then added another measure. Back in his study, with the door firmly shut on the rest of the world, he knocked back half of the amber whisky.

It was futile to waste any more time thinking about her. What he needed to do was work out how to explain to George, and Dafni, in the morning, why she had left.

The view from his window normally distracted him, even at night, when the distant lights of Kefalonia flickered through the dark and the sky was deep and seeded with millions of stars. The magic of it had dimmed this evening.

As a boy he'd loved the holidays he and his little sister had spent on Ithaca. The island, with its peaks, valleys and coves, and the sense of ancient history, which permeated every corner of it had felt like home. His grandparents had always seemed elderly to him, but he'd known they welcomed his presence and they'd given him a freedom that he never experienced in Athens. Returning with George and adapting to living here had been hard, but he thought he'd grown used to it. Now, emptying his glass in another long swallow, he stared into the dark and felt alone.

In the couple of hours he'd spent with Bea he'd felt the stirrings of interest in the world again. Life beyond the stress of trying to be a good father, and running his business remotely, had briefly beckoned and he'd felt lighter. He might even admit that he'd felt happy.

Now he felt foolish for allowing the universe to trick him into thinking things could be about to improve. Nothing was ever that straightforward, and, as had just been proved, it was never going to be as simple as a chestnut-haired woman with grey eyes and a wide smile turning up on the shores of Ithaca.

The regret that tugged at him, at the thought of not seeing her again, felt searing, when he should have simply felt relief. It just showed how starved he was of grown-up, interesting company. *Female* company, he thought, bitterly. Because he couldn't deny the attraction that sparked between them.

It was damned inconvenient. It led his mind astray, to thoughts of what her body looked like beneath that sheer dress; how she'd react if he put his fingers against the pulse at her throat or stroked a thumb across her mouth. He could never have acted on these impulses, even if she hadn't been his best friend's sister. Never, in his life, would he consider mixing business with pleasure. Employees were out of bounds, just as sisters were.

He propped his bent arm against the window frame and leaned his forehead against it, fighting the urge to retrace his steps to the drawing room to pick up the half-empty bottle of Scotch and drink the rest of it here, in his study. Sleep, which was never something he could count on, would not be available to him tonight, so he might as well numb the jagged edges of his frustration and anger with a couple more glasses of the warming spirit.

He dropped his arm and turned from the darkness beyond the window and heard a soft knock on the door.

'Yes?'

For a brief moment, before he could stamp on the thought, hope that it might be Bea flashed through him, prompting a quick spike in his heartbeat.

But the person who tentatively pushed the door open was not Bea. It was Dafni.

She was pale and her voice shook, her words tumbling over each other. 'Something has happened.'

CHAPTER SIX

AT SEVEN O'CLOCK the following morning Beatrice wheeled her bag to the door of her suite and then crossed the room. The windows and shutters were wide open, as they had been all night, but the breeze, which had been cool in the early hours of the morning, now wafted into the room with a warmth that carried the promise of another hot day.

She hadn't even attempted to sleep in the bed. The chair, where she'd spent most of the night curled up, stood behind her, the silk throw cushions squashed and creased. That, she thought, looking at them, is rather how I feel: flattened and in need of refreshing. Guilt and shame had chased through her mind, keeping her awake so that she'd longed for the morning, when she'd be able to escape the force field of energy that surrounded Alexandros. In his presence she felt as if she constantly had to resist being pulled into his orbit if she was to preserve her own will and strength of mind. It would be so easy just to submit to his power. But she hadn't come to Ithaca to lose her independence. She was here to exert it, and she had, to an extent. Now it was time to go.

There was no longer the need to dress like a conservative governess, and she'd stuffed her navy skirt and white blouse into her luggage and put on a pair of comfortable linen crops and a loose cotton tunic. She'd pulled her hair off her face and fastened it into a ponytail with a scrunchie.

She could make out the shape of the ferry chugging from Kefalonia towards Ithaca, a wave curling away from its prow and a foamy wake fanning out behind it. In twenty minutes, it would dock at Pisaetos and she hoped she'd be on it for the return journey.

As she peered down through the trees, the grinding of gears and a faint cloud of dust rising into the morning air were the first signs that her taxi was approaching. If there was any traitorous part of her that muttered in disappointment that the moment of departure really had arrived, she silenced it with a brisk shake of her head.

This was how it had to be: how *she* had to be; sorry for what she'd done but not intimidated by the anger of Alexandros Galatis. *Never* that.

She wheeled her bag along the galleried passage, glancing down into the courtyard where she'd had coffee with Alexandros less than twenty-four hours before. It was cool and shadowed, silent apart from the splash of the fountain in its centre.

The steps of the wide curved staircase were shallow and she carried her bag down with ease. She could hear the taxi engine idling outside. The double doors, which stood ajar, let in a shaft of sunlight that fell in a bright rectangle, giving vibrancy to the warm tones of a patterned rug.

When she was halfway across the hall, two car doors slammed, in quick succession, the tone of the engine changed from an idle to a loud roar and gravel crunched beneath tyres.

Beatrice stopped short as Alexandros Galatis appeared through the doors in front of her.

With the light behind him his face was in shadow, and his expression hidden, but every line of his body—his whole presence—radiated tension. She stepped aside, getting out of his way as he strode across the floor, but when he drew level with her he stopped and half turned to allow her space.

His eyes were etched with fatigue, his mouth set.

'Excuse me.' She was the last person with whom he'd want to engage this morning, or ever, especially as there was obviously some crisis unfolding right here in his life. Briefly, she wondered who it was he'd sent packing, even before she herself had managed to leave. 'I'll wait outside for my taxi.'

But as she stepped forwards his broad hand came to rest on her forearm.

'The taxi has left.'

She glanced towards the door. 'So there must be another one coming for me.'

'No.' He shook his head. 'There isn't.'

She looked down to where his tanned fingers lay on the white cotton sleeve of her tunic. She should step back, away from him, break this contact. Her skin felt heated beneath his palm but a shiver raced up her arm and she felt strangely light and untethered.

'Then I need to…'

'I need to talk to you, Miss Antonini…'

'Capelli. Beatrice Capelli. And no, I don't think you do. I just need to go now. If you, or someone else, could call for a taxi, I'll wait outside,' she repeated.

Finally getting her mind to engage, she moved her arm away from his hand. It dropped to his side, his fingers flexing.

'Capelli, of course. If you'll come to my study…'

'No. We have nothing else to say to one another. You made your opinions of me clear last night, and I don't dispute them. Not for a moment. The quicker I leave, the better it will be for everyone.' *Especially for me*, she was tempted to add but swallowed the words.

'The thing is, I have a problem.'

'I kind of gathered that.' She glanced towards

the door. 'Is your problem the person you've sent away in that taxi, which should have been mine?'

He stared at her for a moment. His hair looked, at some minutes past seven in the morning, as if he'd already dragged his fingers through it fifty times. He lifted his shoulders and dropped them again, blowing out a heavy breath.

'Yes. In a manner of speaking.'

'Who was it?'

'It was Dafni.'

'Dafni?'

'Yes. George's nanny.'

'Then where's George?'

Alexandros raised his chin a fraction and rolled his shoulders. He seemed to exhale some of his tension. Beatrice thought she saw a flash of satisfaction spark in his eyes. He nodded slightly. 'He's in the kitchen where Maria is giving him his breakfast.' He glanced at the watch strapped to his wrist. 'Maria is the cook. He'll be finished in half an hour. If you'll please come to my study, we can have coffee and I'll explain.'

'Explain which part? There seems to be a lot happening.'

'The part about why I need you to stay.'

Beatrice stared at him, pushing a hand towards him, shaking her head. 'That's impossible. You can't want me to stay. Not after what I told you last night.'

'I didn't say I *want* you to stay. I said I *need* you

to stay.' He turned away. 'Please, come with me. We should be having this conversation in private.'

'For me this isn't exactly a conversation. It's more a series of shocks and a totally unexpected demand.'

He turned back, holding up his hands, his palms facing her. 'I'm sorry. This has all happened too quickly and I'm keen for George's day to go smoothly, without a break in routine. If I've come across as rude or demanding, I apologise. Please…' He indicated for Beatrice to follow him. 'I'm sure you would like a coffee?'

Admitting to herself that she might very well kill for a cup of coffee, Beatrice followed Alexandros through the quiet house, up the curved staircase, past closed wooden doors with polished handles and walls covered with portraits of stiff-faced men and women. With a jolt of surprise, she noticed he was wearing the same dark jeans and light-coloured shirt he'd worn the previous evening.

Had he also not slept, like she hadn't? It must have been something other than her revelation about her identity that had kept him from his bed, and she was curious to discover what it was. What had caused the lines of anxiety on his face to deepen? In another universe, would she have been able to soothe them away with her fingers, make his tired eyes close and his breath deepen?

Unhelpful thought! She tried to push it away

and concentrate on why she had to convince him that for her to remain on Ithaca was such a dreadful idea.

He stopped outside a door that bore a small brass plaque with the word *Private* engraved on it. He stood back to let her pass into the room. His big frame took up too much space in the doorway and her shoulder brushed against his chest as she turned sideways to move past him. The beginnings of that curious, heated shiver stirred inside her again and she wrapped her forearms across her stomach, trying unsuccessfully to stop it from blooming, sending warmth flowing through her body, along her limbs, to her fingers and toes.

What was it about this man? In her teenage fantasies, and then later, when she'd planned this, she hadn't ever predicted that the extreme response of her body might turn the tables, and hand control to him. Beatrice looked around, absorbing the atmosphere. There was no doubt at all that this was a man's room. The faint scent of beeswax polish and leather hung in the air. It couldn't be called a man cave, because it was too orderly and serious. Too grown-up. Sunshine from the windows bathed it in light. Her eyes were drawn to the one thing that looked out of place.

On the wide desk in the centre of the room stood a heavy crystal tumbler beside a bottle of single malt whisky. The bottle appeared to be empty and a trace of what had been its contents lay in the bottom of the glass. She felt the heat of his gaze on her and she lifted questioning eyes to his.

He shrugged and shook his head. 'It was a difficult night. Sometimes whisky helps me to relax.'

'Relax? Forgive me for saying that it doesn't seem to have done its job.'

One corner of his tight mouth twitched, and he shrugged. Perhaps he *could* smile. 'I said *sometimes*.' He pulled a mobile phone from a pocket of his jeans and tapped out a message. 'I've ordered coffee.' He put the phone on the desk and seemed about to sit down in the leather swivel chair behind it, but changed his mind, waving towards the chairs by the fireplace.

Beatrice sat in one of them, but Alexandros paced across the floor. When the tray of coffee was carried in and placed on a low table he took the chair opposite her and poured out two cups, passing the milk jug.

'Thank you.'

He inclined his head. 'Dafni received news last night that her elderly mother had fallen ill. She's had to return to Kefalonia to care for her.'

'Oh, I'm very sorry.' Beatrice picked up her cup. 'And so you want me to care for George for a few days, until she can come back? Surely you have staff members who can do that.'

'No, I don't. Not someone who can dedicate their time to him exclusively. Everyone here has a role to play in the smooth running of the house. It's essential for George that his routine continues and he isn't upset or his learning disrupted in any way.'

'He's only four. A few days…'

He held up a hand. 'It won't be for a few days. Dafni has nobody else to care for her mother and anyway she *wants* to be with her. I was able to allow her to go because you are here.'

Beatrice drew in a long breath. 'That's a bold assumption to make. I can't believe you're even considering asking me to do this. You're furious with me, and with Enzo. You doubt my honesty and you said you could never trust me. How can you possibly want me to look after, and teach George?' She shook her head. 'And knowing your opinion of me, I'd feel I was being watched the entire time. Trust is a two-way street, and I couldn't trust you not to judge me.'

Twin sparks of anger, quickly dampened, flared in his eyes. 'Despite your assumption, I can assure you that I don't want you here. But I need you to step into Dafni's place. And I guarantee that I will not interfere with your teaching or question your methods.' He glanced at his watch, again. 'George was already confused when Dafni wasn't there for breakfast. I know he likes you and hopes you will be his new teacher. I also know that you empathise with him.'

'Whatever makes you say that?'

'A simple observation. When I told you that Dafni had left, your first question was not "*why?*" or "*where has she gone?*" It was "*Where's George?*" He was your immediate concern and to me that shows you would put his welfare above everything else.'

Beatrice dropped her head, surprised to see the way her hands were gripped together in her lap. When she looked up again, he was watching her.

'Do I have a choice? What if I refuse?' she said, quietly. 'Will you keep me here against my will? Is this some sort of way to score points off Enzo? Or off me?'

He shook his head. 'This has nothing at all to do with your brother and everything to do with my son. If you were determined to leave, I would never make you stay.'

'You've allowed Dafni to go. You must have been quite sure that you could persuade me to change my mind. What if I hadn't been here? What would you have done then?'

Alexandros turned his head and looked towards the windows. 'I would have refused Dafni permission to go and I would have paid for care for her mother.'

'What? But her mother is ill, and you said Dafni wants to be with her!'

'I will pay for her care, anyway. And if it had become clear that she really needed to be with her, I would have altered my business plans so that I didn't have to travel tomorrow.'

His head turned back and his eyes caught hers. 'And George is my son. Think of him, before you refuse my request.' He leaned forward, folding his arms across his knees. 'Please.'

Beatrice's expression—he had to remember she was no longer Bea Antonini—became shuttered. She'd been animated and indignant at his declaration that he would have made Dafni stay.

He liked the fact that his instincts about her had been correct. She was caring and sympathetic towards others, whatever ill-judged whim had set her on the path of trying to deceive him and upset her brother.

Yes, the previous evening he had been shaken and infuriated by her revelation, and when Dafni had knocked on his study door late last night he'd initially dismissed, out of hand, the possibility of asking Beatrice to stay. To change his mind would demonstrate a weakness on his part, when he'd told her so vehemently that she had to leave immediately.

He'd told Dafni he'd try to work something out, and he'd put the remainder of the bottle of whisky to good use. It hadn't worked its magic, though, and he'd been left pacing the floor into the early hours, exhausted and a little drunk, wrestling with the problems of childcare, the global meeting of his resort managers he was supposed to attend in two days' time and the woman who, presumably, slept upstairs, her rich hair spread across white bed linen, her dark eyelashes brushing her cheeks. Far from wanting sleep, he'd been wired and restless, with the possibility of rest even more remote than usual.

He glanced across at her. Her bent head had caused her ponytail to swing over her left shoulder. If he reached out, he could push it back, swipe his fingers across her curved neck, make her look up at him. He gripped his hands together between his knees.

Admitting to himself that he needed her to stay had been difficult. She'd tried to be dishonest, but her intention was to anger Enzo rather than do any harm to himself. Feeling as he did about her brother, he rather applauded her for that. And anyway, he thought, with a wry twist of his mouth, she'd been absolutely hopeless at lying. Her conscience hadn't allowed her to go through with it for longer than a few hours.

Her hands twisted in her lap while her face reflected the internal battle she was fighting. He was tempted to repeat how important it was for George that she decide to remain, but he kept quiet. He had to allow her to reach her own decision, without further pressure from him.

He may have told her that he needed her to stay, but despite his denial he *wanted* her to stay, too. He just didn't want to examine his reasons. Not too closely, anyway. On the surface it was perfectly obvious that it was the best solution for George, and for himself. But if he dared to look deeper he knew he'd be unhappy with what he discovered.

There was a strange pull between him and Beatrice, which was something completely new to him. He didn't understand it, and he didn't trust feelings he couldn't understand or rationalise. They made him feel insecure and threatened. Growing up, he'd never been able to predict which version of his parents he would meet each day. Trying to please them and avoid their disapproval had felt like walking a tightrope from which he'd frequently fallen.

When his sister had been born he'd discovered how it felt to love someone without reserve. Better still, the love she'd given back to him had been unconditional.

The wild version of himself, to which he'd given free rein as soon as he left home, had been a way of testing his own boundaries as well as those of authority. As his success in the business world had grown, he'd had to curb some of his more extreme appetites, for speed and pleasure; develop a sense of responsibility. With the expansion of his leisure empire came the realisation that others depended on him for their livelihoods, and he'd begun to appreciate the advantages of establishing a more predictable balance in his life. He was ruthless about keeping business and pleasure separate. He didn't like shocks or surprises and this feeling that Beatrice stirred in him shone a bright spotlight on both of those.

The last time he'd felt this out of control and confused had been when that email had dropped into his inbox, telling him that, unless a DNA test proved otherwise, he was the father and only relative of a two-year-old boy in London, called George.

'Did you say you had travel plans?'

Alexandros's attention jerked back to the present, and to the woman who sat opposite him, twisting her ponytail in her long fingers, her grey eyes wide with a question. She'd evidently decided she no longer needed to present herself as a conservative governess. Her linen cutoffs and loose cotton tunic were relaxed and stylish. Despite her lack of make-up and her simple hairstyle, she looked a lot more sophisticated.

'I…yes.' He scrambled to gather his scattered thoughts. He was finding it difficult to concentrate on the things that mattered, although perhaps that was the result of his lack of sleep. Who did he think he was fooling? Not that he found it difficult to concentrate on Beatrice, and wonder if her skin would feel as soft as it looked, and how her mouth would taste under his, if he could kiss her…

'When?'

'*When?*' What was she talking about? Had he spoken aloud? Asked if he could kiss her? He raked his hair back, clutching it in his fist.

'Yes.' She sounded puzzled, which wasn't surprising. He was behaving in a peculiar way. 'When will you be travelling?'

'Um. Oh…possibly tomorrow…'

'That soon?' Through the confusion that fogged his brain, he heard the note of hope in her voice, discordant with the note of alarm in his head. Would she base her decision to stay or go on whether or not he would be here? If he left her with George and went off to Barbados tomorrow, would she ignore all the instructions he'd leave about strict mealtimes, quiet times and learning times? Would she take George swimming without proper supervision, or allow him to stay up late, watching cartoons on TV?

He stood up. 'But on consideration, I've decided to postpone the trip. It can be rescheduled to later in the month and possibly moved to Athens.' *Meaning he need only be away from Ithaca for a day or two.*

'Oh.'

He thought he detected disappointment in the downward inflexion of her voice. 'But that needn't concern you. Whether or not I'm here, George's days follow the same pattern.'

'Except that you wouldn't be there to say goodnight to him. Or read him a bedtime story.'

'I think I mentioned yesterday that Dafni does the reading.'

'But since Dafni isn't here, perhaps this is the time to change that habit. *You* could read to him, without Dafni feeling sidelined.'

'Or *you* could.'

There was a beat of silence before she answered.

'You said you wouldn't interfere with my methods of care and teaching. What if I believe you should read the bedtime story?'

Alexandros rocked back on his heels and pushed his hands into the pockets of his jeans. He stared at Beatrice. She looked perfectly poised now, as if she'd made a decision. The fingers of one of her hands were loosely clasped around the slender wrist of the other. She looked up at him, her gaze steady, and flicked her ponytail over her shoulder with a toss of her head.

He frowned, trying to understand how he'd got into a discussion about bedtime stories, early in the morning, when actually all he wanted to do was to make her stop talking by kissing her.

The thought shocked him, threatening to unbalance him completely. He had to block his thoughts from following these unhelpful and disturbing paths.

Should he reply to her challenge with one of

his own? Did she feel the charged atmosphere in the room, which made him think the air might crackle if he so much as touched her?

'I…might agree. But you'd have to listen, too, to make sure George was happy with the way I read it.'

The silence felt brittle. He was afraid to move in case it shattered into shards and destroyed this moment, which for some reason felt loaded with intimacy. Suddenly he knew, with sharp clarity, that whatever happened next would irrevocably shape things in either a positive or negative way. In his pockets his fingers curled reflexively, digging into the tops of his thighs.

There was a quick, double knock on the door. They both turned their heads towards the sound and then their eyes locked again as they turned back.

'I asked the staff to bring George to me when he'd finished his breakfast.' He took a step towards her and heard her quick intake of breath. Perhaps her poise was not as unshakeable as she'd like him to believe. 'But I still don't know what I'm going to say to him.'

CHAPTER SEVEN

BEATRICE STOOD UP. A young woman, whom she recognised as the server from their dinner the previous evening, came through the door. George walked at her side, clutching her hand.

The woman bent her head and spoke to him in Greek. His blue eyes moved between his father and Beatrice, and he looked unsure.

Alexandros stepped forward and held out his right hand. George copied him, and they shared a formal handshake and greeting.

Beatrice felt as if her heart might crack at the sight of the tentative little boy and his stern-faced father, *shaking hands*. She thought Alexandros loved his son and would do anything to protect him, but he was doing a good job of hiding his feelings. Where was the affection? Why hadn't George run to him, to be swung into his father's arms? Why didn't Alexandros talk to him? Get down to the four-year-old's level? He'd told her George was anxious about Dafni's absence. He should have been reassuring him, asking him if he was looking forward to anything in particular during the day—what he'd had for breakfast, *anything*, for goodness' sake.

It shouldn't be difficult. What was *wrong* with him?

George had turned his wide eyes onto her. His hair had been brushed, but it had sprung back into a golden halo of curls. In his formal shorts, shirt, socks and buckled shoes, he looked out of place and forlorn, as if he'd arrived late for a party and all the other children were already splashing in the swimming pool.

Beatrice dropped to her knees and stretched out her hands to him.

He looked at his father and when Alexandros gave him a nod of consent, George walked carefully across the carpet towards her. She took his hands in hers.

'Good morning, George,' she said, her voice soft and her English words clear. 'I'm very pleased to see you again.'

He looked thoughtful. 'George?' he said slowly.

Still holding his hands, Beatrice changed her position to sit cross-legged on the floor in front of him. 'In English,' she said, 'your name is George. In Greek, it is Georgios. Now, if I'm to teach you English, I'll need to speak to you in English and call you by your English name. George.'

'Will you teach me English?' He repeated his question of the previous day.

'Would you like that?'

Confusion clouded his expression and he turned to his father again, who said something to him in Greek. He looked back at Beatrice, the shadow clearing from his face. Then he nodded.

'Efharisto.'

'Thank you. I'm very pleased. Because I would like it, too.'

Alexandros had moved to stand behind him. She could see his leather sneakers from the corner of her eye. She looked up, and as their eyes met over George's head an unmistakable current of understanding flowed between them.

The line of his mouth softened a fraction and then his head dipped in one brief nod.

Beatrice dropped her eyes and tried to focus on George again. Her pulse rate had climbed to an uncomfortable speed. She felt too warm and a little breathless. She wished Alexandros would step back and give her the space she needed to adjust to the crazy, impulsive thing she knew she'd just done. She'd agreed to stay on Ithaca and be George's tutor, and she'd put herself in the position of having to resist this insane, magnetic attraction to his father, her brother's former best friend.

She could have walked away but she hadn't. She'd fallen under the spell of this lost little boy and in doing so had handed control of her life to the man she'd planned to trick, for the sake of her own revenge.

The trouble she was in now was far more serious than the trouble she'd happily stepped into when she'd arrived yesterday.

It could have been simple, but there was nothing simple about the way she responded to the man who had just become her employer. *That* was super complicated. She didn't understand why he made her feel so…*alight*…and yet she'd willingly committed herself to staying in his presence, so close to the bright flame of attraction which could burn her, like a hapless moth.

But her heart bumped with excitement, when it should have been hammering in trepidation.

Alexandros watched Beatrice gently place George's hands at his sides. She stood up, her long legs unfolding with easy grace. He noticed she'd managed to retreat from him by a step or two.

Relief made him close his eyes for a moment. He hadn't allowed himself to consider not getting what he wanted, but as the tight band he'd felt restricting his breathing slackened, he acknowledged he should not have been quite so sure of himself.

'I'll have a contract printed out for you to sign later today. Do you want to delay beginning your duties until the paperwork has been completed?'

She didn't hesitate. 'No. As you said, it's important that George's routine is not disrupted. We'll begin at once.' She took George's hand. 'Won't we George?' They started towards the door.

'If you'd like to join me on the terrace for breakfast…'

'No, thank you.' Although her voice was firm, he'd seen a betraying flutter at that tender hollow between her collarbones, the quickening of her breathing, her slightly parted lips. 'We'll go to the kitchen and George can help me choose what to have for breakfast.'

Her hand was on the door-handle and Alexandros felt a surge of unfamiliar panic. He wanted to keep her here, with him, for a little longer. Perhaps he should insist that she wait while the contract was prepared. She'd probably refuse… He had to stop these feelings, but since he didn't understand them, he didn't know how.

'Miss Capelli…' Her grey eyes met his, her eyebrows raised. 'Uh…may I suggest that we keep the relationship between us informal…'

'Informal?'

'What I'm trying to say is…' He hadn't been so lost for words since he'd last been hauled in front of his father and berated for dropping three marks in a maths exam. He took a couple of breaths, more to give himself time to reorder his thoughts than for oxygen. 'What I mean to say is, obviously you and I will be meeting frequently, to discuss George's progress.'

'We will?' She tipped her head to the side and her ponytail swung behind her. He was hit by an image of wrapping that long, thick hair in his fist, tipping her head backwards to expose the smooth skin of her throat. He swallowed. 'If you don't want me to change my teaching methods that shouldn't be necessary.'

He pushed his hands back into his pockets, hunching his shoulders. 'Yes. No, I don't mean we'll meet to scrutinise your methods, just to… to make sure George is making progress.'

The look she delivered was level. 'I promise that George and I will get along very well together, and he'll enjoy his lessons. If you stop worrying about him you might be able to rid yourself of some of that tension you're holding in your muscles.' Her voice dropped and there was genuine concern in her tone. 'You must be exhausted.'

Yes, he thought, *I am*. He rarely admitted to feeling tired, and to have someone else notice and seem to care made him feel *seen*. And vulnerable. He had to fight that. Somehow, she had taken control, and he needed to wrest it back. He made another effort to get the right words out. 'What I want to suggest is that you…and I…should be on first-name terms. It will make for a more relaxed environment…'

She nodded. 'As you wish, Mr Galatis… Alexandros. Please call me Beatrice. George will, too.'

'Alex,' he said. 'I'd like you to call me Alex.'

'Alex?' She paused. 'That's what my brother calls you. I might find it difficult.' But she nodded and led George out of the room.

The door closed behind them with a soft click. He dragged in a long breath. The trace of her floral fragrance lingered on the air, incongruous alongside the scent of leather and furniture polish, which had characterised the room for generations.

He started towards the windows, intending to push them wide, to invite in a morning breeze that might help to clear his head and also the reminder of Beatrice, but he stopped, acknowledging that he didn't want to remove the traces of her presence from his sanctuary.

He swore under his breath. What had he even been thinking? He should have made some other arrangement, although he was clean out of options. Taking a break from work was impossible and restarting the recruitment process for a tutor would take up time he didn't have.

He just wished Bea...*Beatrice*...didn't make his breath hitch every time he saw her teeth close over her soft bottom lip and make him want to stop her doing it, in case she hurt herself. That her wide grey eyes didn't rest on his son with compassion and a look of deep understanding, making his own heart twist with the pain of the fact that George would never know the love of a mother. That all his blood hadn't surged south when he caught a glimpse of the smooth, golden skin, and the shadowed hint of a cleavage, when she knelt on the floor in front of George.

That she wasn't the little sister of his former best friend, and that he'd sworn he would never, ever touch her.

The fact that her brother had broken their pact and married his sister didn't mean he could break it, too. On the contrary, he would always be the bigger person. He'd demonstrate his integrity and iron will. He'd never give in to this…temptation.

He flung himself into his desk chair and turned on his computer, forcing himself to concentrate on sending an email to his PA in Athens, asking her to send Beatrice's employment contract to him. Then he informed her he could no longer travel to Barbados and would need the meeting of his managers to be held in Athens, at a time to be decided.

He'd told himself he couldn't leave Beatrice alone with George because she couldn't be trusted, but he knew that wasn't true. It was obvious that George's welfare would be her main priority.

The fact was that he didn't want to leave Beatrice, at all. He didn't want to leave her, but he didn't know how he was going to tolerate being with her, either.

CHAPTER EIGHT

BEATRICE SETTLED GEORGE at the table in the kitchen, while Maria prepared his lunch.

'I need to speak to Mr Galatis. Do you know where I might find him?'

Maria wiped her hands on her apron. 'His lunch was served on the terrace a little while ago. But—' she shook her head '—he does not like to be disturbed.'

'That's a risk I'll have to take.' Grateful that she'd learned enough Greek to communicate, Beatrice headed for the door.

'I'll be back before you've finished your lunch, George. I need to talk to your daddy about our shopping trip.'

She found Alexandros sitting at the table on the terrace with his back to her, facing the view. His hair was damp and tousled. It curled a little, just above the collar of his linen shirt. He must have showered and changed after their earlier meeting.

A mobile phone was clamped to his right ear and as she stepped over the threshold onto the tiled terrace she heard him speaking loudly in Greek. It was too quick for her to understand, but he sounded angry. She hesitated and drew back but she wasn't quick enough. He must have heard her because he twisted round, looking over his shoulder.

She held up a hand in silent apology, and began to turn away, but he shook his head. In a few staccato words he finished the conversation and clicked the phone off as he put it down on the table. Then he stood up, turning fully towards her.

Her brother had never commented on his friend's stature and so she'd been unprepared for the way he simply commanded the space around him, with the air of someone who took the fact for granted. As she approached him, she pushed her hands into the pockets of her linen crops, trying and failing not to think about how hard and yet smooth the planes of his chest might feel under her palms.

His brow was furrowed. 'Is something wrong?'

'Not exactly.' She shook her head and dragged her wayward thoughts back into line.

His brows lifted. 'Not exactly? Well then what *exactly* is it that you want, Beatrice?' He glanced down at his phone. 'I was on a call…'

'I…' It was the first time she'd heard him use her name in full, and something about the way he said it suffused her in a liquid, warm glow. It sounded soft, almost like a caress from his lips and she wanted him to say it again just so she could be sure she hadn't imagined it, or the delicious effect it had on her.

Get a grip. It's just your name, which you've heard a million times before...

She bunched her fists in her pockets and pulled her shoulders back, lifting her chin.

'I apologise for disturbing you, Mr Ga... *Alex...*'

One corner of his mouth ticked up and she felt heat begin to spread over her cheeks.

'Was that difficult?' Was he mocking her? His eyes crinkled a little at the corners. No sign remained of the anger she'd detected in his voice, moments earlier.

'I...yes, it was. But... I expect it will become easier with practice.'

'Ah. So you agree that we might be meeting frequently, to talk about George's progress? That would provide you with the opportunity for *practice*.'

There was no doubt about it now. He was definitely winding her up. Beatrice had tried to kill her habit of nibbling at her bottom lip when she felt stressed or unsure, but she found she was doing it now. She'd have to try harder, especially if it caused his dark eyes to focus on her mouth with that unexpected intensity.

She released her lip and touched the tip of her tongue to the place she'd nipped.

His eyelids dropped and she heard his quick, sharp intake of breath. He closed a fist around the back of the chair next to him, the knuckles of his hand gleaming beneath the stretched bronze skin.

The air between them thickened, throwing up an invisible barrier, which she knew she must never cross, and yet it would be so easy to take a step forward and stretch out a hand…

No. The distance between them was negligible, but it might as well be a mile. She had to maintain it. She made that a rule, effective immediately.

'Possibly,' she said, keeping her voice level with a determined effort. 'But what I need now is your permission to take George shopping.'

If she'd said she planned to take George on a rocket into space she didn't think she could have surprised him more.

For a few long seconds he looked as if her words were completely incomprehensible. His brows pulled together, the lines deepening between them.

'Shopping?'

'Um, yes.'

'Shopping for what? He has absolutely everything a four-year-old boy could possibly need. More than everything.'

Except for unlimited warmth and affection from the one person in the world who should be giving it to him.

'And you've only been with him for a morning. How can you know what he needs?'

'Well, I've had a quick look through his closet and he doesn't seem to have any suitable clothes.'

'What do you mean? He has clean clothes every day.'

Something of the anger she'd heard in his voice a minute ago had crept back. He was turning this into a challenge.

'Yes, I'm sure he does.' She nodded, keeping her voice even. 'Clean clothes of the sort he is wearing. But they're not suitable for a Greek island summer. They're too formal, warm, restrictive. *Dull.* He needs bright T-shirts and cotton shorts. Sandals or plimsolls. Clothes he can run about in.'

'Well, I don't think I've ever seen him run.'

'My point exactly.' Beatrice threw up her hands and saw him track the movement with what looked like fascination. 'He needs to learn to express himself, and not just in language.' How could anyone be so lacking in insight? 'I've only spent one morning with him, I know, but he is much too reserved for a four-year-old boy. He only speaks when spoken to, never volunteers anything.'

'My parents would consider that a definite plus.'

'Oh.' Beatrice hesitated. But she'd come this far and wasn't inclined to back down. 'I wouldn't want to contradict your parents, but I'm here to teach George and to do that successfully I need him to feel more relaxed—less afraid of messing up.'

'And, in your opinion, different clothes will help him to achieve that?'

She dug her nails into her palms to stop herself from saying something she might regret. 'Yes. I do think so. It's difficult to relax when you're not comfortably dressed.'

'I've only ever bought him the best…'

Remembering, too late, that interruptions made him irritable, she butted in anyway.

'I'm not criticising the quality of his clothes. I can see they're expensive and that's part of the problem. George is probably afraid of getting paint on them, or jam…'

'Paint?'

'Yes, when we do painting, which I was planning to include in his lessons tomorrow. We'll go into the garden and choose flowers for him to paint. Or perhaps a tree.'

'I thought lessons happened in the schoolroom. Not the garden.'

'Lessons do happen in the schoolroom, but not all of them.' Her patience was wearing thin. 'And we agreed that you would not interfere with my teaching methods. So to get back to my original question, may I take him shopping?'

'Mm. Okaaay.' It sounded as if he was far from

okay with the idea, as if he simply didn't understand, or thought she was being unreasonably picky. He rubbed a hand across the back of his neck. 'Anything else?'

'Yes. I couldn't find any swimmers, either. Are they kept somewhere else? The pool house?'

His face cleared. 'That I can explain. George is afraid of the water, and I haven't wanted to push him.' He rocked back on his heels, looking satisfied. 'He doesn't need swimmers.'

'George is at the perfect age to learn to swim. Everyone should be taught how to be safe in the water, especially in a climate like this, and where there is the sea or a swimming pool everywhere you look.' She spread her arms wide to embrace the sun and the sky. 'By keeping him away from the water you're doing him a disservice, and one which could prove dangerous…'

She stopped to draw breath, suddenly aware that she was on the verge of a rant. But this was a subject she felt strongly about, and she risked becoming fierce in the expression of her insistence. Alexandros…*Alex*…now looked more annoyed than confused.

Well, she'd lied to him, planned to trick him into believing in her assumed identity. He had every right to be annoyed with her, and to mistrust her intentions. But this wasn't about her, it was about George, and if she was going to tutor him she had to get his father to agree to her suggestion.

'It has never been my intention to withhold anything from him that could be beneficial. I hoped that his fear of water might lessen as he grew older, but so far…'

She took a deep breath, dropping her voice in an attempt to sound less accusatory. 'These feelings are likely to become more intense if this is allowed to continue.'

'Yes.' His penetrating gaze was focussed back on her now. It dropped from her eyes to linger on her mouth and then moved down to where she knew her cotton top would be rising and falling with her accelerated breathing. 'Yes,' he murmured, again. 'I can see that.'

The heated silence between them suddenly felt charged and dangerous, and suspicion hit her like a thrown punch. Was he no longer referring to George and swimming lessons? She fought the urge to wrap her arms across her chest, or to look down at her body, but if she did he'd know she'd read the subtext of his words. Pushing her fists back into her pockets, she locked her elbows, and her shoulders jumped up around her ears.

'So…' The word caught in her throat. She swallowed and tried again. 'So, does that mean I have your permission?'

'Permission? Beatrice…'

Despite her acute discomfort, she registered

the fact that the way he uttered her name still sounded like a soft, unhurried embrace. Somewhere amidst the hammering of her heart and the taut silence, she felt thankful.

'Permission to take George shopping for some new clothes. Please.'

'It's not necessary to take George shopping. Tell me what he needs and I'll order everything from Athens. I can make a phone call this afternoon and the order will be delivered early tomorrow morning.' He shrugged. 'In time for him to wear his new clothes for your *painting* lesson.'

Beatrice dropped her shoulders and tried to keep her cool. There was no point in getting heated, but he set her nerves jangling. If she pushed him too hard, too fast, he might simply refuse and walk away. She needed to persuade him in a reasoned, calm manner, but she was close to losing her composure.

'That would be very convenient, of course, but don't you think George would benefit from an outing? Learning to choose things, and that they must be paid for, would be a useful experience. He'd need to try on shoes, too, before I buy them.'

'I'll order several sizes and you can send back the ones that don't fit him.'

Trying to sound regretful, when she really wanted to plead with him, she resorted to her last hope: mild emotional blackmail.

'Yes, of course that's a possibility. He'll be disappointed, though. I told him I was coming to ask you for permission. But I'm sure I can find a way to soften the blow.' She turned to go.

'Wait.' The word snapped behind her, and she paused. '*If* I agreed, where would you go?'

'Oh!' She looked back at him, mentally punching the air. 'I've done a little online research and there's a children's shop in Vathy that I think will have the few things he needs. I thought we could go later this afternoon, after his nap. Could Iannis drive us?'

Alexandros watched Beatrice turn on her heel and cross the terrace. He was becoming familiar with the sensation, not unlike loss, which ambushed him every time she walked away from him. Although how could something, or someone, feel so familiar after a mere twenty-four hours? Each time it happened, he had to consciously steel himself against going after her. If he lost that battle, what would he do or say when he caught up with her?

Please come back, because being with you makes me feel... What did it make him feel? Her hips swung a little as she walked. The tip of her ponytail brushed the space between her shoulder blades and her hair briefly sparked with chestnut fire as she passed through a shaft of sunlight.

Being with her made him feel... If he was going to be brutally honest with himself, it made him remember that he hadn't had any female company for much too long. And now wasn't the time to change that. She was his best friend's—*ex*–best friend's—sister and his son's tutor. If he'd been looking for an unsuitable woman, she was right here, in his house, in his space, where he rarely tolerated anyone for long.

He'd never felt a strong need to discover anything much about the women he'd dated. There was only so much you could learn about someone in a single night. So this feeling that he wanted to know everything about her was perplexing. What difference could it make to him if he knew her favourite colour? Or what she might choose to snack on, late at night? How she liked to be held? Or kissed?

Furious at the direction his thoughts seemed programmed to take when he didn't consciously hold them in an iron grip of denial, he turned to face the view again. He glanced at his phone where he'd discarded it on the table when Beatrice—God, he *loved* her name—had appeared. He'd have to call Stavros back in Athens and finish the conversation, but he'd lost the impetus of the discussion and no longer felt like talking to him. He'd send him an email, instead.

He sat down and pushed the remains of his lunch around the plate, his appetite gone, going over their conversation in his mind. As a child, he'd been taught to only speak when spoken to, but was that how he wanted George to be? No, it wasn't. The fact that his parents would approve should be a massive red flag. Just because he'd been forced to wear a formal school uniform didn't mean he should perpetuate the habit with George. It had taken Beatrice to make him realise he was doing all the wrong things. He felt caught on the back foot and he didn't like the feeling, at all.

Should he have agreed to let her take George into Vathy? Allowing his son to leave the property without him made him feel anxious. He always knew exactly where he was, and what he was doing, even if he himself was on the other side of the world. That was the advantage of a strict timetable. It kept George safe and stopped him from worrying about him, quite so much.

He'd undertaken not to interfere with Beatrice's way of teaching, but she'd only spent one morning with George. How did he know she'd take proper care of him?

You've read her CV. Her testimonials. Of course she'd take proper care of him.

Anger at Enzo rolled over him. This was all his fault. If he'd been honourable, and not broken their pact, none of this would have happened. He reached for his phone on the point of calling him and telling him, again, what he thought of him, but he stopped. He refused to lower himself to the level of trading insults, if Enzo even answered his call. He was probably still sunning himself somewhere on his honeymoon, not giving a thought to the hurt he'd inflicted on his little sister.

That hurt, Alex realised, was what made him angriest of all.

If he refused to allow them to go shopping, Beatrice would accuse him of being obstructive and of interfering. And she'd be right. He could try to explain that the thought of George leaving the grounds without him made him uneasy. Although he couldn't overstate the enormity of the initial shock of discovering that he had a two-year-old son, he'd come to regard him as a precious gift that he didn't deserve. A cruel stroke of fate had robbed George's mother of her life but had, at the same time, delivered George to him. What was to say that a similar blow might not take him away again?

It would probably appall Beatrice to learn that the only time his son had left the Villa Eirini had been when he'd taken him, in his own jet, to meet his parents in Athens. The visit had not gone well and he was in no hurry to repeat the experience.

The feelings of anxiety he associated with that memory made his stomach churn. He rotated his shoulders, trying to relieve the stiffness in his muscles and wished he didn't care that his parents disapproved of him, and of George.

He was a man who made decisions and moved on. He rarely questioned himself, and yet here he was, doing just that. Beatrice seemed to soften him, make him doubt that he was…*right.* Then he had an idea that was so simple he couldn't believe he hadn't thought of it immediately. It made him feel better at once.

He would tell her that Iannis was not available to drive her and George to Vathy for their shopping trip. But that he was.

CHAPTER NINE

HEARING THE SOUND of a vehicle approaching the front of the Villa Eirini, Beatrice took George's hand and stepped outside.

The afternoon heat had started to fade as the sun began its descent into the western sky, and the warm air was heavy with the scent of the blowsy blooms of the ancient rose that scrambled up the façade of the house.

Beatrice hitched her canvas tote bag higher onto her shoulder and looked in the direction of the approaching car.

But it was not Iannis in the Jeep that rounded the side of the villa. Shc stepped back as a silver Porsche SUV, with tinted windows, stopped in front of them.

The driver's door swung open and Alex leapt out. He pushed up his sunglasses and rested a forearm along the top of the door. The gold signet ring on his little finger gleamed in the sun.

'Ready?'

'Yes…we are. Only I wasn't expecting you.'

She couldn't hide her surprise. 'From your reaction to my suggestion earlier I got the impression that you don't like shopping.'

He lifted a shoulder. 'I do so little shopping, I hardly know how. I decided I should learn alongside George, if you're willing to teach me. And Iannis has taken the *Penelope* for an engine service this afternoon, so he couldn't drive you to Vathy.'

Beatrice narrowed her eyes against the glare of the sun behind him. She couldn't make out his mood.

'I'm not sure there is much, if anything, I could teach you, Alex.' She swallowed. She'd managed to say his name without a hitch in her voice.

'I don't think I agree with you. Not at all.' His voice dropped. 'But shall we see?'

She wished she could take her words back. She felt that annoying and frustrating blush creeping up her cheeks and bent her head so that her hair, released from its ponytail, swung across her face. She needed to stop allowing him to make her feel so…*aware*…of him and so attuned to the tone of his voice.

Her plan all along had been to *pretend* to Enzo that she'd fallen in love with Alex.

George was looking up, his eyes moving between them. He looked as confused as she felt at the unexpected appearance of his father in the place of Iannis.

'How lovely, George, that your papa has come to take us shopping.' Turning to Alex, she lowered her voice. 'It would be good if you said this is going to be a fun outing for both of you, even if you don't enjoy shopping.'

Alex's eyes widened. 'You're probably right,' he murmured, then he bent to speak to George. The boy nodded and the anxiety faded from his face. Beatrice felt his tight grip on her hand slacken.

'And what about you?' Alex returned his attention to her. 'Will it be fun for you?'

'Of course it will. Especially since I've told George we can have ice creams afterwards. I discovered there's a café by the water, so we can watch the boats, as well.'

'Mm. Sounds…perfect.' His mouth twitched in a half-smile. 'Shall we go?'

He picked George up and swung him into the child safety seat that had been fitted into the car, strapping him in and closing the door. Beatrice followed him around to the passenger side.

He cupped her elbow in the palm of his hand and helped her up into her seat. His skin felt cool but even though his touch only lasted a few seconds, that betraying current of sensation fizzed along her nerves. Her stomach hollowed and tightened and she rubbed at her elbow with her fingers.

Alex slid into the driver's seat and pulled his seatbelt across his chest, clicking the buckle closed. He tilted his head to look at her, his eyebrows raised.

'Seatbelt, Beatrice.'

'Oh, yes, of course.' She tugged the buckle down and fumbled with the fastening, staring ahead through the windscreen. Then she felt his fingers brushing against hers as he guided the buckle into the slot. She drew her fingers away and folded her hands in her lap.

Perhaps it was the intimacy of the closed, warm space that made her so aware of how near they were to each other. She looked over her shoulder to check on George, hoping she looked more relaxed than she felt. He was swinging his legs and looking out of the window.

'I can tell from the safety seat that George has been in this car before. He seems quite relaxed.'

Alex pulled his sunglasses down and nodded. 'Yes, he has. A couple of times. But not for a while.'

The sight of his hands, firm and yet relaxed on the steering wheel, made her feel strangely secure, as he guided the big car down the sloping driveway. He nodded towards a track that branched off to the right, curving downwards through the trees. 'That's where you would have come up with Iannis, from the quayside.' At the touch of a button, the ornate iron gates at the end of the drive swung open and he turned onto the narrow twisting road.

'So you've taken him on other outings? Where have you been?'

She fixed her eyes on the road ahead, determined not to look at the way the muscles of his thigh flexed beneath the dark fabric of his jeans as he braked or accelerated.

'Not outings, exactly. It was a trip to introduce him to my parents, in Athens. It was his third birthday and I thought it would be a good opportunity for them to meet him. We took the ferry across to Kefalonia and then flew from there.' He glanced in the rearview mirror and then quickly across at her. 'It wasn't a fun trip.'

Beatrice returned his glance. 'I'm sorry. What went wrong?'

His laugh was dry. 'It would be safe to say pretty much everything, starting with the fact that I'd had a son I knew nothing about.' He slowed for a bend in the road, then accelerated up a hill. 'I'm not close to my parents. I seem to have disappointed them with most of the things I've done, and George was apparently one of my more major mistakes.'

'They could hardly blame you for not knowing of his existence if his mother never told you.'

'That wasn't how they saw it. It was confirmation, if they needed it, that my whole lifestyle is corrupt and that I'm only concerned about myself. I thought they'd be pleased to meet their grandson, and they were kind to him, but in a patronising way. They made it very clear that they were not pleased at the unconventional way he arrived in my life. Or in theirs. No baby shower. No effusive announcement in the press.' The car crested the hill and he braked, pulling to the side of the road. 'I didn't follow the rules. But then, I never have, really. That's always been the problem.'

'Oh. *Oh!*' Beatrice's gasp of surprise was at the vista that was spread out below them. The small town of Vathy lay around the edge of a bay. The whitewashed walls and red ochre tiles of its buildings gleamed in the sunshine alongside the sapphire blue of the sea. Green-clad slopes reached down to the water, curved around on both sides, forming a sheltered anchorage. Beyond lay the northern part of the island, its shores receding into the distance between the sea and the deep sky.

'So beautiful,' she breathed.

'Yeah.' He nodded, his voice soft. '*So* beautiful.'

Beatrice turned to explain to George that the town he could see was where they'd buy his new clothes, and their ice creams, but her eyes met Alex's instead. He wasn't admiring the view, at all.

Alex watched George's eyes grow round as Beatrice handed him the ice cream he'd chosen. It was a swirl of strawberry pink in a waffle cone, topped with a whole, fresh berry. He reached out and took it in both hands, inspected it carefully and then popped the strawberry into his mouth.

His attempt to say 'thank you' around a mouthful of strawberry was garbled, and Alex and Beatrice both laughed. To Alex's surprise, George laughed, too. His little chuckle was blurred by a mouthful of pink ice cream, as he gave his full attention to eating as much of it as possible before it began to melt.

Alex hadn't expected to enjoy this shopping trip and he wasn't sure at what point it had become fun. But sitting at a café table, shaded by a red-and-white-striped umbrella, watching George eat ice cream, was definitely one of the best things he'd done for…well, for as long as he could remember, in fact.

He almost wished he'd decided to have an ice cream himself. He lifted his bottle of water, cracked the cap and took a long drink. Beatrice had chosen a salted caramel cone, and he watched, mesmerised, as the pink tip of her tongue appeared between her lips and swirled around the creamy mixture.

'Mm, that's *so good.*' She closed her eyes and shivered in mock ecstasy. 'Are you sure,' she asked, blinking at him, 'that you don't want to change your mind?'

His fist tightened around the plastic water bottle. It gave a little under the pressure and made a soft creaking sound. He took another long sip and shook his head.

'No, thank you.' The only thing he wanted to change his mind about was keeping a safe distance from her. They weren't even one day in, and he didn't know how he was going to manage for the next however many weeks she stayed. How long would it be before he stopped imagining the taste of salt and caramel on her lips?

Perhaps Dafni's mother would stage a quick and unexpected recovery and Dafni would return to rescue him. But far from being comforting, the idea filled him with dismay.

George looked happy in a way that he'd never seen him look happy before. There was ice cream on his face and sticky drips of it tricked over his small hands. He looked as if he was having the best time of his life.

Alex's wondered how Beatrice had brought about this change in him so easily. Why had he ever waited for an outsider to treat his son to ice cream on the beach? He should have done it himself, a long time ago. It was such a simple thing.

Two bags of shopping sat at their feet. Between them, Beatrice and George had chosen striped shorts in three different colours, and plain T-shirts to go with them. Then Alex had decided more T-shirts were needed and had added one in every colour to the pile on the counter. Sandals that wouldn't mind getting wet were fitted onto

George's small feet, and his formal, buckled shoes and socks packed away in Beatrice's tote bag, along with his other clothes.

It had all been easy and stress-free, and then they'd walked along the path that curved around the bay to this café. The owner had recognised him and greeted him effusively, and for once being recognised hadn't annoyed him. He hadn't even minded when the waiting staff cast speculative glances at Beatrice and George and spoke to each other in low voices. He didn't care what they surmised. Perhaps they thought they were a family…

That thought stopped him in his tracks. He'd made the decision a long, long time ago that he'd never be a part of a family. In his experience, the purpose of a family was to put pressure on each other, to do better, be richer, be seen in all the right places and find a suitable wife or husband.

Like it or not, his sister was married now. He hoped his parents were happy to have Enzo for a son-in-law. He was certainly rich enough for them. But with her daughter settled, his mother would ramp up her efforts to marry him off to a suitable woman. Finding an heiress who'd be prepared to take on another woman's child would be challenging for even her legendary networking skills. He shook his head. It was never going to happen.

He wanted none of that pressure. He'd made

his own way, succeeded beyond the wildest expectations of most people on the planet, pushed himself beyond his own limits and survived, but they wouldn't approve of him until he'd done the conventional thing. They'd missed the opportunity for a big flashy wedding for their daughter, and that left him firmly in the spotlight.

A wail from George brought his attention crashing back to the present. A blob of ice cream had toppled off the cone and dripped down the front of his new blue T-shirt. His face crumpled in distress and his bottom lip trembled, his eyes filling with anxious tears.

'Oops. Alex, please hold this for me.' Beatrice handed her cornet to him, picked up a paper napkin from the table and wiped the ice cream off George's T-shirt. 'It's okay, George. Eating ice cream wouldn't be nearly so much fun if it wasn't messy.'

She dug in her tote bag and pulled out a packet of wipes, using several to gently clean George's sticky hands and face.

Alex shook his head. 'What else do you have in that bag, Beatrice?'

'I was the one who suggested ice cream. I came prepared.'

She sat back and took her cone from his fingers. 'Thank you. That's better, George. Finish up and then let's see if you can count the boats.' She squinted at her ice cream. 'Did you steal a lick?'

'Maybe.' He shrugged. 'And there're far more boats than he'll be able to count.'

'That doesn't matter. Next time he'll be able to count more.'

'Next time? Do you mean you're going to need to go shopping again?'

'No, but we don't have to go shopping to have ice cream on the beach. This is fun. Aren't you enjoying it?'

'Yes.' His response was slow. 'I am. I didn't think I would, but I am.'

Beatrice handed him a wide smile. Her eyes danced.

'I didn't think you would, either. I think you only came to keep an eye on me, although I have no idea what trouble you thought we might get into without you watching us.' She popped the pointed end of the cone into her mouth, crunched it between her teeth and sighed. 'And has Iannis really taken the *Penelope* for an engine service?' She licked her fingers and Alex looked down, rolling the water bottle between his palms.

'He has.'

'Well, I don't blame you for not trusting me. I didn't do myself any favours, did I?'

'No.' He shook his head. 'You didn't. But George responds very well to you, and he looks happier than I've ever seen him. I have to give you credit for that.'

'Thank you. Why do I feel that your approval is not given lightly?'

'Because it isn't.' He picked up a paper napkin. 'You have a smudge of caramel on your chin. May I?'

She took the napkin, her forehead creasing. 'No, you may not.' She rubbed at her chin with it and then scrunched it up in her fist. 'But thank you for pointing that out.'

Alex leaned back and stretched up his arms, linking his hands behind his head. He studied her from behind his dark shades. Her mouth, which had given him such a beautiful smile, had turned serious. She didn't want him touching her and she was quite right. He shouldn't *want* to touch her.

But, God, he did.

She'd left her hair loose this afternoon and now she pushed it away from her face, gathering it up in her hands and twisting it around, before letting it drop again. It flowed through her fingers like molten silk, falling over her shoulders so that the ends brushed the place where the swell of her breasts rose and fell beneath her tunic.

'I'm sorry. That was presumptuous of me.'

'What's presumshish?'

He looked at George in astonishment. He didn't think he'd ever asked him a question before. If Beatrice was surprised, she wasn't showing it.

'If you do something another person might not

like without asking them, it can be called presumptuous.'

George nodded, apparently satisfied. He started counting, ticking the numbers off his fingers but eventually ran out of numbers that he knew. 'Too many boats,' he said.

'Ah, but look, there's one very big boat.'

Alex followed the direction of Beatrice's pointing finger. A superyacht, gleaming silver and white in the sunshine, had cruised into the bay and was dropping anchor. The blue-and-white Greek flag fluttered at the stern.

George stretched his arms wide. 'It's this big.' He wriggled off his chair.

'You can go down to the edge of the water if you like. We'll be right here.'

'I think he's spoken more in the last five minutes than he has in the last two years.'

'He understands a great deal. He just needs to build up his confidence about speaking, in both Greek and English. It's much easier in an informal environment like this, doing something fun, than sitting at a table in the schoolroom. The teacher-pupil relationship is blurred.'

'I didn't see how it would make a difference, but you're clearly right.'

'Thank you.' Beatrice half turned in her chair. 'My brother has one of those.' She was looking out at the superyacht.

'Yes, I know.' He leaned forwards, removed his

shades and propped his folded arms on the table. 'We once partied on her for a week. Non-stop.'

Her eyes whipped back to meet his. 'You were at *that* party?'

For a heart-stopping moment he thought she was going to say she'd been there, too. It had been seven days fueled by exorbitant amounts of alcohol and several beautiful women. His recollection of the week was hazy, but the pain of the come-down afterwards was seared into his memory. He wasn't proud of his behaviour at that time of his life and he rather badly didn't want Beatrice to have been a part of it.

'Yes, I was, in body, but my mind was absent for a lot of the time. Were…you there?'

'Me? No! Enzo would never have let me near a party like that. Or *any* party he threw.'

Alex released a long breath. 'Good. It didn't end well.'

'No. I remember that the reports made the gossip columns. There was a mention of the police. I saw pictures.'

He grimaced. 'So did my parents. It confirmed their opinion of my lifestyle and my friends. When I took George to meet them they asked if he'd been conceived at that party.' He remembered the acute shock he'd felt at their blatant question, but then how he'd had to concede that they'd been justified in asking it although not, in his opinion, in requesting such intimate details. But then, they'd never pulled any punches.

Beatrice's questioning grey eyes were on him.

'Was he, Alex?' Her voice was barely above a whisper.

He shook his head. 'No.' Relief smoothed out the anxiety on her face. 'Not there.'

'Did you care for her?' she asked. 'Even for a little while?'

He wanted to say yes. He thought that was what she wanted to hear and knew it would cast him in a better light, but it wouldn't be the truth.

'No. I wish I could say I had. But I've never wanted a lasting relationship. They turn sour, make people bitter and unhappy; trapped. I've always been clear about that, and I've always been…so careful. I don't know how it—George—happened, and I never will. But I can't regret it, because George is the best thing that's ever happened to me.' He shifted on his chair, uncomfortable with the frankness of the conversation. He'd never admitted that fact to anyone before. He didn't know why he'd done it now.

There was something about Beatrice that made him want to open up and examine feelings he tried to keep locked away, because if he allowed them oxygen and light, they could come alive and wreak havoc with his precarious peace of mind. Regret, which he felt about missing out on the first two years of George's life; guilt about the fact that in order for him to raise his son, his mother had had to die; and the always present anxiety that he wasn't doing things right.

Once that trio of stressors got to him it could be days before he managed to wrestle them back into the part of his brain where he locked them up.

Beatrice's eyes were soft. 'If George is the best thing that has ever happened to you, you need to learn how to celebrate it more.'

Beatrice looked up from the pages of the storybook. George had finally settled, and his breathing had become regular.

He'd fought sleep, but eventually his eyes had grown heavy. She put the book on his nightstand where he might find it and try to read it himself when he woke in the morning. Then she stood and looked down at his sleeping form. His hair curled, slightly damp, around his forehead and he slept with the side of his face resting in the crook of his arm.

At least, she thought, she had clear memories of both her parents, right up until the moment of the cable car crash. George might never remember his mother at all. Since he'd been knocked unconscious in the accident that had killed her it was unlikely he'd have a memory of that, either.

He'd lost so much. His mother, his home, everything he knew had been obliterated in the few seconds of a driver's inattention. It wasn't surprising that he'd found it difficult to verbalise anything, for a long time. She at least had Enzo, although right now it felt as if she'd lost him, too.

She clicked off the reading lamp, leaving just the pale glow from a teddy bear–shaped night-light on the chest of drawers. As she turned, tucking her hair behind her ears, she saw Alex, arms folded across his chest and one shoulder propped against the doorframe.

He pushed himself upright to let her pass. He smelled of cedar and citrus and warmth. Up close, she could see the evening shadow of stubble, which roughened his chin and jaw.

'How long have you been here?' She ducked her head, keeping her voice low. 'Or were you planning to read to him?'

'Long enough to enjoy the story. You read it far better than I ever could.'

'You could recite the alphabet to him, and he'd love it, because it was you.'

'The alphabet would get boring very quickly. For George.'

'Papa?'

Alex rolled his eyes. 'We've woken him.'

'It won't be for long. He's had a tiring day—getting to know me a little, going out. Ice cream! Just say goodnight to him, as you always do. He'll be out like a light in a minute or two.'

She left him and walked away, down the dim passage. Lingering twilight glimmered beyond the ancient dimpled glass of the windows, casting distorted shadows across the rugs and wooden floor. The house felt timeless, and Beatrice imagined that if she stopped and held her breath she might hear echoes of long ago whispering along the walls.

But she picked up her pace, wanting, and yet not wanting, to reach the corner in the corridor, which would mean the sanctuary of her suite was within reach.

She didn't quite make it.

'Beatrice?' She stopped, putting one hand on the wall beside her and waiting for him to catch up. The cool plaster beneath her warm palm felt soothing. She had to be ready for whatever it was he wanted to say.

'As you predicted, he fell asleep again almost at once.'

She nodded. 'Good. He was very tired, and a little over-excited.'

'You must be tired, too. Last night and today have been stressful. You've handled it all with admirable grace.'

'It's kind of you to say so. I don't think you slept much last night, either.'

His eyes narrowed. 'What makes you say that?'

'This morning you were wearing the same clothes as last night. Just a little more…rumpled.'

He half smiled. 'Come downstairs and have a drink with me. We can celebrate your first day.'

'Does that mean you're no longer angry with me?'

'I wouldn't go that far. But let's say my position could change.'

'And mine?'

'Yours is assured.'

Beatrice dropped her hand from the wall and leaned on the windowsill, cupping her chin in her hands. Keeping her back to him felt more secure. That way, she didn't have to see the way his eyes darkened when he focussed on her, or watch the muscles of his jaw tense.

The encroaching darkness had rubbed out the line between the land and the sea, leaving the distant lights of Kefalonia floating in the blackness.

'Do you wish Dafni back?'

'No.'

The deep certainty of his voice made her shiver, even though every cell of her body felt alight with the awareness of him standing close behind her. Too close for safety, and yet not close enough. What would she do if he decided to close the gap? A part of her wished that he would, but she wouldn't know how to respond to him, if he did.

'I thought this afternoon's outing might have been too disruptive. Perhaps you prefer Dafni's predictable regime.'

'I thought routine and predictability were best for George. Dafni has been good with him but seeing him with you…you have something more.' She thought he'd moved closer and she tensed.

'The letter of recommendation from the school where you teach mentioned your obvious love and understanding of children and your particular empathy with any child who has experienced trauma. Is that why George relates to you so well, do you think?'

Only their breathing broke the silence. The moment felt rare and precious and she wanted to prolong it, but Alex was waiting for an answer.

'I understand how it feels to lose a mother—both parents. I *remember* it. The shock and bewilderment were indescribable. Dislocating. In a few moments my whole life changed forever. I couldn't move forward or begin to heal until I could accept its new shape.'

'I'm sorry.' There was a rough edge to his voice. 'You must have heard those words so many times that they must sound empty, but I do mean it.'

She shook her head. 'No. It's never wrong or too late to say them. It was people who said nothing that hurt the most.'

'How could anyone not feel sympathy for a grieving child?'

'I learned that most people were uncomfortable with grief and so I hid it. It was years before I realised that refusing to confront it wouldn't make it go away. It isn't something you get over, or leave behind. You grow around it so it becomes a part of who you are. When I accepted that, I began to be more comfortable with it and now I wouldn't want to change it. Perhaps that's why I have empathy with anyone who has suffered a loss.'

She stopped, regretting being so open. Many people were unwilling to talk about loss and grief. She didn't want Alex to be one of those, but he didn't walk away as she feared he might.

'What about Enzo? He never wanted to talk about it.'

'I was an adult before I thought about the fact that he was only eighteen, about to start university, when he became my guardian. He'd always seemed grown up to me. The responsibility must have been overwhelming.'

'He sent you to boarding school, in a foreign country. Surely you resented it?'

'No. I was only eight and I didn't question his decision. I became determined to try to do everything right. Somehow I felt being good would keep me safe. I always tried to do what he wanted, which is why it hurt so much when he secretly married Thaleia, as if I wasn't important enough to tell. And why I did what I did to hurt *him*. It's the reason I'm here.'

'Small consolation, but they didn't tell *anyone*.'

'I know that now, but at the time… I realised I wasn't going to be treated as the exception.'

The silence felt weighty. She rested her forehead on the window, her breath fogging the glass.

'You're…you *are* exceptional, Beatrice. You don't seem to harbour any bitterness…'

'Bitterness?' She turned her head. 'What would be the point of that? It wouldn't bring my parents back. I'm lucky. I have a life many people would envy.' She heard the rasp of Alex's palm as he dragged it across his jaw. His arm brushed against her shoulder as he moved to stand next to her.

'I've rescheduled the global meeting of my managers for two days' time.'

She turned her head. His face was in shadow, but his profile was visible against the pale wall of the window recess. 'Where will you be going?'

'Athens. Will you be alright?'

'Of course.' When he returned, she'd be cooler, a little more distant, not reacting to him like a teenager in the presence of a rock star. The last two days had been a rollercoaster ride of deception, uncomfortable truth, changing plans and then accepting that she needed to stay. Alex being absent for a few days would give her time to regain her equilibrium. 'I'd like to order some more English storybooks for George, if that's okay.'

'Email a list to my PA. I'll bring back what I can.'

'Will you be away for long?'

'Just a few days. There'll be two days of meetings, and I need to schedule time to see my parents, if they can fit me in.' He paused. 'About that drink?'

Beatrice pushed herself away from the window and shook her head. 'I don't think that is a good idea.'

'Once again, Beatrice, you're probably right.'

If the light had been better she thought she'd have seen him half smiling.

CHAPTER TEN

IT WAS LATE afternoon by the time Iannis brought the *Penelope* alongside the jetty below the Villa Eirini. It had been an intense day. After his morning meetings he'd met his parents at a restaurant for a lunch which had gone on for much longer than he'd planned.

He'd been ready to leave from halfway through the first course, but they'd insisted on ordering two more, and then coffee. He'd refused the liqueurs and left them at the table, sipping at their Metaxas and sampling the complimentary chocolates, looking disappointed. Nothing new.

His father had queried the wisdom of him living on Ithaca, again, ignoring his argument about it being the best place for George, and his mother had wanted him to commit to attending a fund-raising event in the autumn. His presence, she insisted, might induce other attendees to flash their cash in the form of larger donations. Also, she hinted, it would be the perfect opportunity to meet an eligible woman in search of a rich husband.

He'd agreed to donate a large sum of money to what he was sure was a worthy cause, but refused to attend.

'You will be at your father's birthday party, though?' His mother had taken his hand as he'd bent to kiss her cheek. 'Bring George, of course. It's time he was introduced to our friends.' Her laugh was brittle. 'Some of them don't actually believe we have a grandson.'

The date had completely slipped his mind and perhaps to make himself feel less guilty about the charity event and to speed up his escape, he'd agreed.

He could have returned to his penthouse, with the view of the Parthenon, to change out of his business suit, but he'd asked his driver to take him straight to the airport where his jet was waiting. On board, he'd shed his jacket and tie, then sat, drumming his fingers on the cream leather seat, impatient for the hour-long flight to Kefalonia to end.

It seemed to take Iannis forever to make the mooring ropes safe, fore and aft, but at last they drew up in the Jeep, in front of the villa. The fiery heat of the day had softened to an all-enveloping warmth, which brought out the scent of the wild herbs growing beyond the driveway. Finally, he felt he could breathe again.

He grabbed his bag, slammed the Jeep door behind him and strode into the house.

The Villa Eirini had always been quiet. It was one of the many things he loved about it. Returning from Athens, or from wherever he'd been in the world, he could be sure that the cacophony of foreign cities, airports and hotels had been left behind, and he could relish the silence and peace he found within the ancient walls of his home.

He wasn't sure why he'd expected this time to be different, or why the silence felt somehow deafening. He paused his stride, halfway across the hall, to listen.

Had he thought he'd hear George's voice, or his footsteps? He never had before. Perhaps he was still having his *messimeri*? He glanced at his watch and frowned. George's nap should have finished half an hour ago. Then he reminded himself that Beatrice might have changed the order of things.

He put down his bag in the study, dropped his heavy silver cufflinks on the desk and rolled up his sleeves. Then he headed for the housekeeper's office, next to the kitchen.

Thea, his housekeeper, leapt to her feet from behind her desk. 'We weren't expecting you until this evening, Mr Alexandros.'

'I managed to get away earlier. Do you know where Beatrice and George are?'

'At lunchtime she mentioned they planned to go swimming after his quiet time.' She smoothed her hands over her skirt. 'Again.'

'Again? They've been swimming before?' He managed to stop himself from adding *without me*.

'Each afternoon. Yes. In the pool.'

'Thank you.' He'd already turned to go, tossing the words over his shoulder.

Trepidation swamped him, questions hammering in his brain. Had Beatrice forced George to go into the water, when he was afraid of it? Surely she wouldn't do such a thing. But she'd said he needed to get over his fear as soon as possible, or it might grow worse. How would she have persuaded him to go swimming? Would he—*should he*—approve of what she'd done?

The peace he'd anticipated was immediately shredded by anxiety. He should never have left George with Beatrice when he knew so little about her. Guilt staged a jail break and took up its habitual position on his shoulder, along with the certainty that he was doing everything wrong.

He took the marble steps down from the terrace two at a time and jogged along the paved path through the gardens towards the pool enclosure. It was one of Iannis's tasks to check the security fencing and gate every day, and to maintain the pool. Beatrice must have persuaded him to give her the key.

Increasing his pace as the anxiety mounted, he found the gate had been left open. Another rule breached. He stepped through it and pulled it closed behind him.

Shock hit him in the chest like a kick from a horse.

George stood on the curved marble lip of the pool, at the shallow end. His arms were stretched out, his golden curls plastered to his head and he didn't look terrified, at all. There was a wide smile on his face and, as Alex stared, he began to count.

'One…two…'

Alex lunged forwards. 'George, *no*!'

'*Three*.' The small boy launched himself into the air and plunged into the water, right in front of where Beatrice stood, waist-deep, holding her arms out to catch him.

He disappeared beneath the surface for a breath-stealing second, then came up, laughing, in her arms.

It had all happened so quickly he didn't think they could have heard his shout, but Beatrice turned, with George's legs around her waist, and his arms around her neck.

'Papa!' called George. 'Watch me again.'

Still carrying him, Beatrice waded to the curved Roman steps and began to climb out of the pool. When she reached the side she put George down, took his hand and walked towards him.

He felt a sudden constriction in his chest. The two of them looked carefree and completely at home. In his suit trousers, leather shoes and formal shirt he felt out of place. When had he become an interloper at his own swimming pool?

'Alex, you're back early.' Her voice was cool and calm. 'We've been having a wonderful time. George can swim a few strokes on his own.'

Alex tried to match her demeanour, but his racing heart wouldn't play the game. He took a couple of deep breaths, his mouth drying up.

George was fine. Happy. Yet *he* was a wreck. He drew a hand down over his face and pushed his fists into his pockets.

'Are you okay?' There was an undercurrent of concern and confusion in Beatrice's voice. Her eyes caught his but he looked away. 'You're not angry, are you?'

'No. No, I'm not angry.' He wished he could down a glass of iced water, or, better still, a cold beer. Along with his mouth his throat was parched. 'This is just…'

The sight of George enjoying the water was startling, but something—*someone*—else altogether had caused his lungs to squeeze and his heart to pound against his ribcage. She was standing right in front of him, wearing a lipstick-pink bikini, water sluicing down her long, shapely legs, trickling between her rounded peaked breasts and dripping off the ends of her bright hair.

He didn't think he'd ever seen anything more beautiful in his life, and he wanted her, with the mindless desperation that comes with wanting something you know you absolutely cannot have.

'Just…?'

'Unexpected,' he managed to grind out. 'I'm… surprised. That's all.'

He pinched the bridge of his nose between his thumb and forefinger, trying to buy time, to get himself at least looking as if he was as cool and controlled as she sounded.

'Good.' Beatrice looked down at George. 'We wanted to surprise you, didn't we, George? Why don't you come for a swim, too?' This time when her eyes met his he read a challenge in them. 'George can show you his swimming strokes.'

'I…no.' Alex shook his head. 'I have work to do. Emails to deal with. Perhaps another time.'

Swimming with Beatrice wasn't something he would be doing anytime soon. No way could he be in the pool with her until he'd tamed his physical responses, but he had no idea where to begin. His brain might be telling him she was beyond reach, for every sensible, morally correct reason in the universe, starting with his honour and finishing with the practical problem of her being an employee, but his body had gone into full rebellious mode.

Had he ever felt such an uncontrollable surge of desire? He wasn't a teenager, awash with raging hormones. He kept his needs and appetites safely compartmentalised and strictly rationed and when he wanted to satisfy them, he did so, on his own terms.

George looked up at him and he reached out to push the wet curls off his forehead.

'I'd love to see you swim, but maybe next time.'

He turned to leave, but not quickly enough to avoid seeing the flash of disappointment in his son's blue eyes. He'd failed him and he'd also failed to meet the challenge Beatrice had laid down. They'd been having a joyful afternoon, and he'd spoiled it, like a dark cloud coming in front of the sun. Perhaps he should have stayed away longer.

Beatrice tucked George into his bed and bent to study the books on the shelf, trying to decide what to read to him. She pulled out a book of English nursery rhymes, but when she straightened up Alex was at the bedroom door. He'd changed into hip-hugging black jeans and a black T-shirt. In his arms he carried a pile of books.

'I managed to find some of the books you asked for.' He put them on the table. 'I've ordered the ones they didn't have.'

Surprise made her hesitate. Since her encounter with him at the pool she'd felt uneasy. He'd seemed cold and preoccupied and she wondered if he'd decided he didn't want her looking after George, after all.

A few days ago, she'd wanted to be sent away,

but now she desperately wanted to stay. During the three days Alex had been in Athens she'd made steady progress with her new pupil. He was speaking much more, in both Greek and English, beginning to make observations about his surroundings and tentatively expressing some of his likes and dislikes.

'Oh, thank you.' She ducked her head and tucked her hair behind her ears while she recovered her composure. She picked up the first book and smiled. It was an English translation of *The Odyssey*, written in comic strip form, with colourful illustrations. 'This is the perfect way to introduce George to the history of Ithaca. Thank you!'

'Before I went away you suggested that I might read George's bedtime story.'

'Of course.' She handed the book to him and indicated the chair. 'Is it okay if your daddy reads to you tonight, George? He's brought some wonderful new books from Athens.'

George's eyes widened, and he nodded.

At the door Beatrice turned back to look at him. His serious eyes were fixed on his father. She felt a little tug of emotion in her chest. This was what she wanted to happen—for Alex to engage more with George and to try to build a more affectionate, fatherly relationship with him, but the sight of him opening the book in his hands while his son watched intently gave her a strange sense of loss. She'd begun to love being with George.

Her job was to provide an environment in which he could thrive and learn. She wanted what was best for him and she must not make the mistake of growing too attached to him. All pupils grew up, moved on and jobs came to an end.

She returned to her suite intending to catch up with emails, but not reading to George made her feel that she hadn't finished her day's work. Settling down to answer emails or picking up her book didn't appeal.

The temperature had dropped a little, but the room was warm. She opened the tall windows, but the slight breeze that stirred the curtains did nothing to freshen the atmosphere. The air felt thick and a little humid. She ran her fingers through her hair and lifted it off her neck, securing it in a messy bun.

Trying to concentrate in the heat was impossible. Alex's cool manner when he'd found her at the pool with George bothered her. She felt as if she'd overstepped some invisible line he'd drawn, and offended him, but unless he was willing to explain the problem she couldn't put it right.

His manner when he'd arrived in George's bedroom with the new books had been formal. She searched for the connection they'd had before he'd gone away to Athens, but somehow she couldn't re-establish it in her mind. She thought she'd managed to seem cool, even though seeing him again so unexpectedly had shaken her.

Her determination to keep her response to him controlled had failed at the first glance, but he hadn't appeared to notice the fast beating of her heart or the way her breathing had become shallow and quick. As if to prove to herself that she could deal with this she'd suggested he go swimming with them.

If he'd taken it as a challenge, he'd been right, but the challenge had been more to herself than to Alex.

She stripped off her clothes and looked around for her sarong to wrap around her body before taking a shower. The brightly printed length of cotton was nowhere to be seen, and she knew she must have left it by the pool. She had a clear memory of draping it over one of the sunbeds.

Her pink bikini hanging in the bathroom was almost dry. She quickly wriggled into it, pulled on shorts and a T-shirt, and slipped out of her bedroom door. George would be asleep by now and Alex would be working in his study.

Swimming a few laps of the pool would calm her overworked mind and cool down her body. The cycle of interrupted sleep that had established itself during Alex's absence might even be broken.

Alex closed the book and added it to the pile on George's nightstand. He reached out and brushed his fingers over his son's flushed cheek and George stirred, a hitch interrupting his soft, regular breathing. He stood up with extra care, being as quiet as possible.

Dinner would not be served for another hour. Usually, he spent this time answering emails and making calls. Apart from keeping in touch with the luxury resorts he owned around the world, in an historic building like the Villa Eirini there was never an end to the list of tasks that needed attention to keep it in the pristine condition he demanded.

On a normal evening, when he was satisfied that he'd cleared his desk as much as possible, he would sit on the terrace with a glass of chilled Sauvignon Blanc, as the last of the light faded, and think about the following day. He liked to pre-empt surprises and be ready for any problems before they arose.

Since Beatrice had arrived, the concept of normal no longer existed for him. Not a single aspect of his usual routine appealed to him. A restless energy sapped his concentration and when he reached his study he stared at the list of emails in his inbox and switched off the computer without answering any of them.

There was nothing, he decided, which couldn't wait until the morning. But unless he managed to unravel the cause of his irritation, he knew tomorrow would be no better than today. Mild panic stirred in him. He had to deal with this, before mild became acute.

The schedule he'd set himself and his managers in Athens had been punishing. There'd been too many meetings in too few days, three working dinners, which had gone on late into the night, and then the lunch with his parents, at which he'd had to try to be civil. He knew they'd be rolling their eyes and shaking their heads as soon as he left the building.

All he'd wanted was to be back here, wrapped in the quiet orderliness and security of his home. He could have anything he wanted in the world. He'd been familiar with how easy it was to buy pleasure, and how many people were anxious to pay him attention because of who and what he was. None of that mattered anymore. The peace of mind he craved, knowing that George was safe and asleep upstairs, could not be bought.

And, the insistent voice in his head repeated, knowing where Beatrice was, too. He'd told himself he was impatient to see George when he'd returned home in a rush this afternoon, but who was he kidding? Where George was he'd known he'd find Beatrice.

The encounter with her in George's room had been deliberate. He could have kept the new books for the following day. They would have provided an opportunity to discuss them with his son and decide which he'd like to read first.

He'd been anxious to reset the atmosphere between Beatrice and himself, after interrupting George's swimming lesson in such a clumsy way.

But after her obvious pleasure at the new books, she'd withdrawn.

He wanted to know how she'd managed to encourage George to conquer his fear of the water. He remembered the confusion in her eyes when she thought he was angry, and he wanted to put that right.

Now there was no way of seeing her again this evening, short of knocking on her door, and he dismissed that idea before it had even half formed. What if she asked him in… What if she didn't?

He balled his fists, relishing the pain of his fingernails pressing into his palms. The muscles of his shoulders and arms bulged with tension and a headache began a silent throb behind his right eye. He usually looked forward to this time of peace in the place he loved more than anywhere else in the world, but Beatrice had brought a disturbing energy to the house. On one level he resented the disruption to his ordered life, but on another he couldn't deny that it excited him.

It wasn't the sort of energy he needed right now to deal with problems that arose, every day, somewhere in his empire. It was the sort which made him wonder how it would feel to have her fingers probe his rigid muscles and massage out the knots of stress and whether he'd ever get enough of her scent, however deeply he breathed in.

Was this how it felt to be driven insane by temptation?

He could never, ever touch her. He was an honourable man whose word was steadfast and the vow he'd made to Enzo ironclad, even though Enzo had broken his side of the pact.

And one touch would never be enough. With an instinct he didn't know he possessed, he recognised that, like a drug, one touch of her fingers on his skin, or his mouth on her lips, would drag him into a cycle of addiction that several lifetimes would not be enough to cure.

Odysseus had wanted to hear the call of the Sirens even though hearing it would lead him to destruction, so he'd commanded his men to tie him to the mast of his ship to prevent him from jumping into the sea.

There was nobody he could ask to help him overcome this longing.

He needed to keep as much distance between them as possible, but he didn't want to. Somewhere he had to find the strength of mind and character to resist.

Never had the gap between what he should do and what he wanted to do been wider. Anger flared through him, fueled by the recognition that it was entirely directed inwardly, at himself.

Beatrice could not be held responsible for the way she made him feel. He was at fault and the only safe way he could think of remedying the situation was to send her away.

What sort of man did that make him? Would

he really dismiss the one person who had been able to make his son happy, because he couldn't rely on being able to control himself? Was he really so weak that he couldn't trust his own body to obey his mind? Frustration made him want to pound something, very hard, until he felt better.

He could go down to the gym in the basement to run ten kilometres and go five rounds with the punch bag.

He could send an email to Dafni asking her to come back as soon as possible and then start the tedious process of finding a tutor for George all over again.

The only certainty in his world was the fact that he was not going to do any of those things.

The change in George was startling. He was happy and engaged and obviously adored Beatrice. He may not approve of her teaching methods, but he had to admit that they were a success, so far. He would never sacrifice his son's happiness on the altar of his own desires.

Going on past experience, this desire for Beatrice, if he acted on it, would last for twenty-four hours, tops. One steamy night in her bed would be all he needed to rid himself of this inconvenient and all-consuming longing.

What would he do then? Give her the ferry fare, or her airfare back to Geneva? He couldn't give her the one-night stand talk about no commitment, no second date, no exchange of contact details.

He'd have to continue to see her every day, interact with her over George's progress, *see her in that pink bikini in the pool…*

He tried to breathe. The atmosphere in the room was oppressive and he turned for the door. If he didn't get a breath of fresh air, he'd go mad even more quickly than he already was.

The drawing room was lit by a single shaded lamp on the table behind one of the sofas as he strode through it and out onto the terrace. The table was laid, ready for dinner and the glass candle lamp glowed in a warm pool of light. Although he hadn't eaten since lunchtime, he wasn't hungry.

Low-set solar lights glowed beneath the lavender edging, lighting the garden paths. He walked quickly, shoulders hunched, head bent, with no plan of where to go, and when he slowed up he was in the olive grove on the slopes beneath the villa. The inky sea stretched to the horizon, punctuated by the dim lights of yachts and a ferry ploughing its way towards Kefalonia.

He half wished he could be on it, heading for somewhere—*anywhere*—else.

As his breathing slowed and grew quieter, he became aware of the rhythmic, soft splash of someone swimming.

CHAPTER ELEVEN

BEATRICE HAD SWUM five laps before she found a sustainable rhythm. She'd started fast, sprinting as if she had to shake off something at her heels instead of pacing herself. Each time she turned her head to inhale, her breath was a sharp pant.

Instead of calming her it was adding to her agitation. She had to slow down. It wasn't easy to force her arms to take regular, smooth strokes and her legs to kick with an unhurried beat but as her breathing eased into an even pattern, synchronised with her body, the soothing effect of the repetitive exercise began to take effect.

As her mind focused on swimming, the agitation lessened, and she relaxed.

Slicing effortlessly through the warm silky water, the anxieties fell away, giving her the mental space to think more rationally.

Her sole purpose on Ithaca, at the Villa Eirini, was to teach English to George and help to build his confidence. If the fact that she was employed by Alex annoyed Enzo, so much the better. But her initial plan, to pretend to fall in love with Alex, no longer held any attraction for her. George needed stability and attention. The way he'd responded to her over the past few days had been extraordinary, and she was fizzing with ideas about how to build on the progress they'd made. She had so much to give him, and the rewards he gave her in return, in the form of smiles, laughter and a growing enthusiasm for everything they'd done, were rich.

She would not risk spoiling it all by acting on the deep, visceral emotions Alex aroused in her.

Because if she did, she'd have to leave.

A voice in her head argued that she'd be leaving, anyway, at the end of the summer. That was something she couldn't bring herself to examine, yet.

One of her prime rules was to maintain a healthy and professional distance between herself and her pupils and their families, but the isolated, personal nature of this job made that more difficult. She identified with George's loss of his mother. She knew how frightening it felt to grow up without the protection of parents who loved you unconditionally. There was no doubt that Alex loved his son, but their relationship was formal and distant, and he was often away.

Just as she had been when her parents died so suddenly, George had been wrenched from the life he knew and taken to a strange country, where the language and people were foreign. At an age when he was not yet able to communicate properly, he must have been frightened, confused and bewildered. She longed to help make things easier for him.

She wanted him to learn that he didn't have to try to please everyone all the time, to be accepted or earn approval. It was okay to make mistakes and important to discover that the grown-ups were not always right. It was normal to feel sad sometimes, or happy. Neither emotion needed to be hidden.

How could she achieve these things if she made the monumentally stupid mistake of falling for his father? Alex had made it plain that he didn't believe in relationships. Relationships trapped you, he'd said. He'd spent his childhood trapped in a family where attention was given in proportion to achievement or compliance. His freedom had been hard to win. It was too precious to give up.

If she invited him into her life—her *bed*—he'd most likely accept. After all, Enzo had broken their oath so why shouldn't Alex? There was nothing for him to lose. But at the end of the summer, there would be two hearts hurting on Ithaca. She would be devastated to say goodbye to George and she thought he'd be sad, too.

As for Alex, *his* heart wouldn't even be dented.

Alex didn't want to startle Beatrice—it could only be her in the pool—so entered the enclosure quietly and closed the gate behind him carefully.

But, hell, if she suddenly found him watching her she was going to be just as startled as she would have been by the sound of the gate. He hesitated on the paved path that led across the mown lawn to the marble surround of the pool.

It was not fully dark and the only sound was the gentle lapping of the water against the tiled sides. Beatrice had stopped swimming and turned to float on her back. The pool gleamed with the pearlescent sheen of mother-of-pearl inside a seashell. He could barely make out the shape of her body just beneath the surface, her pale skin covered by the darker pink triangle shapes of her bikini. Her hair floated around her head in a dark halo.

He should leave. If he moved carefully, he could get through the gate and into the shadows of the garden without her seeing him. She need never know he'd been watching her, but that felt wrong. Underhanded. She was entitled to privacy, but he'd already violated it. He was not entitled to spy on her.

In the gap between knowing he must announce himself and deciding how to do it, at the same time upsetting her the least, the silence was broken.

'Alex.' Her voice was low, and she continued to float, motionless. 'I heard the gate.'

'Beatrice.' His throat was dry.

With a supple movement she rolled over and

swam a few strokes towards the steps, then began to wade out of the water, silver droplets running off her like liquid diamonds. She walked towards him and he tensed, ready to back away, but she stopped beside a sun lounger. She gathered the wet weight of her hair in her hands and squeezed the water out of it, tipping her head to one side. Then she picked up a wrap, which shimmered like silk in the dusky almost dark.

Spreading the fabric between her outstretched arms, she wrapped it around her glistening wet body and tucked the end in at the front. Alex saw damp patches spread out on it where it touched the fabric of her bikini.

He folded his arms across his chest, gripping his biceps in his fingers, and bit his lip. Hard.

'I left this here this afternoon.' She glanced down at the wrap and smoothed her hands over her hips. 'I decided to fetch it, and to have a swim.'

He nodded. 'A good idea to cool off. It's a very warm evening.' He forced his eyes to move up from her body, to rest on her face.

'Yes.' She raised her head. 'And I needed to… think.'

'Swimming helps you do that?'

'It does. And running, too. But it's too hot for running.'

'You could use the gym in the basement. It's air-conditioned.' Did he actually have a death wish? If he encountered Beatrice in the gym, running on the treadmill, probably wearing tight Lycra, his blood pressure might rocket to somewhere dangerous. As if in warning, his heart picked up speed.

'Oh. Thank you. But the pool…' She turned her head to look at the tranquil water, with marble surrounds, lush grass, and jasmine scrambling over the fence, its scent almost overpowering on the night air. 'I love the pool.'

Her eyes, velvet soft, met his. He felt as if every breath he took reeled him in closer to her. He could stop, if he broke eye contact with her, but something outside his control, stronger than his will, kept them connected. He could make out the rise and fall of her chest, and he was sure the pulse at her throat must be beating faster, to match the pumping of his own heart. The shadowed hollow between her collarbones looked soft and vulnerable, and he needed to put his fingers there, just to experience how she would feel beneath their touch.

He reached out but found her cheekbone instead. He ran the pad of his thumb along it, his fingers slipping into her wet hair, above her ear, his palm cupping her jaw.

Early morning dew on a rose petal, he thought, wildly, stroking again with his thumb. His other hand landed lightly on her shoulder.

'Beatrice.' Her name was barely a whisper on his lips.

She turned slightly so that her mouth brushed the base of his thumb.

'Mm.'

A jolt of sensation rocketed through him at the touch of her lips on his skin and his fingers flexed against her scalp.

Then his thumb found her soft, full bottom lip. It trembled a little, beneath his touch.

Her hands came up to land on his chest and he bent his head, resting his cheek on her wet hair.

'I want to kiss you,' he murmured, tracing small circles in the drops of water on her shoulder, then slipping his arm around her, spreading his hand across her back.

He felt the tension drain from her body as she relaxed against him, dampness seeping through her wrap and onto his T-shirt and jeans. Something unfamiliar and tender unfurled beneath his breastbone and a sense of release flowed through him as his hand strayed downwards to the small of her back, pressing her against the length of him.

'I want you to.' Her voice was husky. 'So much. But…' He felt her shake her head against his chest and her narrow shoulders shuddered under his hand.

He took a stuttered breath of his own and for

a minute their mingled, rough breathing was all he could hear on the night air.

'But this is wrong.' Finally, he finished her sentence for her. 'I know. You're Enzo's sister and George's tutor. It's wrong, on both counts.'

'Enzo…' Her voice was muffled against his T-shirt, but he heard the catch of hurt.

'If Enzo hadn't broken our vow, you wouldn't be here. We wouldn't be doing this.' And yet he couldn't regret it.

She tipped her head back to look up at him. Her mouth was so close to his that later, when he relived these moments, over and over again, he didn't know how he'd stopped himself from claiming her lips and allowing himself to sink into oblivion in her arms. Her eyes held a sheen that he hoped was simply a reflection of the starlight because he couldn't bear the thought of her being sad.

'Do you want me to leave?'

'No.' There was a thread of fierceness to his voice that he hadn't intended her to hear. He shook his head. 'No,' he said, more gently. 'This afternoon I saw how much George loves you and how much you're helping him. I don't want to spoil that.' He took an unsteady breath. 'And I…'

'If we…if you and I…do this…it'll spoil it anyway. Because it's not what you want. Not really.'

'Oh, it is. But I—I'm afraid I'd end up hurting you.'

He couldn't remember ever considering that he might hurt someone, before. But there was something so open, so honest, about Beatrice, that he felt compelled to say it.

She eased away from him and he let his arms, which ached to band around her and fix her against him, drop to his sides. The gap between them felt like a gulf. She bent to pick up her bundle of clothes from the sunbed and she wriggled her toes into her flip-flops. He thought she shivered, and he had to stop himself, again, from putting his arms around her.

'Are you going swimming?' She straightened up. 'I'll go now, so I won't disturb you.'

'No. I'm not swimming. Do you want to get dressed?' He nodded towards the pool house, its marble columns shrouded in darkness.

'I'll go back up to the villa. I need a shower. I'm sorry I made your T-shirt wet.'

'Don't be.' He swiped his hands over his face. 'Beatrice?'

'Yes?'

'Have dinner with me?'

She pulled her bottom lip between her teeth and shook her head. This time there was no doubt at all that she shivered. 'Thank you. But I think we might both regret it if I did.'

After several minutes under the stinging hot shower her shivering began to subside, but her skin glowed pink and smooth before the episodes wracking her body eased completely.

She turned off the taps and stood, wreathed in steam, resting her forehead against the tiled wall. In the unlikely event that she ever ran a marathon she imagined the aftermath might feel something like this. Her legs trembled and her arms felt weak. The strength she'd needed not to kiss Alex and not to beg him to kiss her, and then not to cry, had made her eyes and throat ache.

A part of her wished that when she'd asked if he wanted her to leave, he'd said yes. But then she thought of George and the way he was learning to trust her, going from being afraid of the water to flinging himself off the edge of the pool into her arms, and she knew she would do whatever she could to stay.

If staying meant avoiding Alex, she'd have to learn how.

She would not allow the fear of what she was beginning to feel for Alex to compromise the progress she'd made with George. She had to subdue her own feelings in order to protect him.

It should be easy, so why did it feel as if she was hanging onto her willpower by her fingernails? If she—if they—gave in to this insane, all-consuming attraction that burned between them, the person who would suffer the most was an innocent boy who'd already endured the trauma of losing his mother.

Standing in the privacy of her bathroom, it was easy to be logical. But then she wondered if Alex might be taking a shower, too. Was he standing under a torrent of water, rivulets running over his hard pecs and rigid thighs, with his eyes closed and that square, rough jaw clenched, determined to wash away the need, which he'd labelled as wrong?

The fact that it was wrong didn't make it easier to ignore.

She might try to avoid Alex, but they'd still see each other every day. Falling for him for real would be the payback for thinking she could pretend.

CHAPTER TWELVE

ALEX'S DETERMINATION TO avoid Beatrice lasted less than twenty-four hours.

The morning after almost kissing her, he'd been convinced he could do it. He resolved to limit himself to his bedroom and private sitting room, and have his meals served in his study. He issued an instruction that he should not be disturbed, except in an emergency.

By midday, he was almost climbing the pale ochre-coloured walls.

They hadn't even kissed, and yet he couldn't get her out of his mind. He'd been in the habit of walking away from his brief encounters with women without a backwards glance. What, in the name of every Greek god, was happening to him?

He told himself that this agitation was because he wanted to see George. The relationship he'd started to build with him had only become possible because of the way Beatrice was breaking down the barriers of his shyness and lack of confidence. Seeing his son happy and smiling, beginning to communicate, felt addictive. He wanted to get to know him, more and more, and to see how he was opening up to new experiences with less anxiety.

But where George was, Beatrice would be, too.

Could he compromise and allow himself to see her during the day? His staff members were constantly visible, in and around the villa and gardens. It would be necessary to maintain a strict code of conduct in public, and he'd make absolutely sure that there were no private moments.

George's bedtime would be awkward. Reading to him had felt like the most precious time he'd ever shared with him and he was determined to make that a part of his evening routine. Increasingly he realised what a distant, undemonstrative figure he must seem to his son and how effective Beatrice's methods of coaxing him out of his solemn, almost-silence were proving to be. Changing the way he interacted with him was difficult. Expressing and showing his feelings did not come naturally to him, but he had to change that and he counted each small step as a victory.

He was standing at the open windows of his study, in the late afternoon, bargaining with himself about when or how he could see, or avoid Beatrice, when he heard the magical sound of a child's laughter.

He leaned forwards, searching through the trees. Beatrice and George sat on a blue-and-yellow-checked rug in the shade of the ancient mulberry tree at the edge of the lawn. She'd tucked her legs under the skirt of a soft, flowing sea-green dress. Her hair was twisted into an untidy knot on top of her head and as she raised a hand to turn the page of a book on her lap he caught the glint of silver bangles on her wrist.

George pointed at the new page and Beatrice nodded. Then he clambered to his feet and ran towards the flower border. He was wearing a pair of his new shorts, a blue T-shirt and his feet were bare. He stopped and appeared to be searching for something, then he bent to pick a flower and ran back to stand in front of Beatrice, holding it out for her to see.

Even at this distance, Alex felt warmed by her smile of delight.

He pushed the heels of his hands into his eyes. He should back away, return to his computer and the emails he'd so far failed to answer.

Grateful that no one could hear the word he uttered as his resolve shattered, he left the room.

Beatrice didn't hear Alex's footsteps as he approached across the grass and she looked up in surprise at George's exclamation of 'Papa!'

He stopped at the edge of their rug, his hands pushed into the pockets of his jeans, his dark hair mussed.

All day, she'd been reliving the feel of his

thumb brushing her cheek and then her mouth, the gentle pressure of his palm across her shoulder blades and in the small of her back, hearing the husky need in his voice, which had made her shiver even as warmth spread through her.

'Alex.' She heard the wariness in her voice and knew it would shadow her eyes, too. 'I…we… didn't expect to see you here.'

'I heard you from my study window.' He glanced over his shoulder in the direction of the mansion. 'I wanted to see y—what you're doing.'

'We're playing a game about plants and flowers.' Beatrice pushed a stray lock of hair off her forehead. 'It's in one of the books you brought from Athens.' She held the book out towards him. 'Look.'

Alex squatted down next to her. A hint of the citrus and cedar notes of his cologne, another reminder of their almost kiss, made her take a deeper breath.

'We look at the picture and then George searches for the flower.' She waved a hand towards the profusion of plants and flowers that grew along the edges of the lawn. 'Then we compare it, learn its name and he copies it.' She pointed to a page covered in George's colourful drawings.

'That's excellent, George.' He sat down on the rug and looped his arms around his bent knees. 'No swimming lesson today?'

'We're about to go to the pool. Would you like to swim with George?' Beatrice stood up, brushing petals and grass from her skirt and packing up the books and crayons. 'If I'm there he'll probably have the confidence to go into the water with you.'

Two afternoons later, George finally leapt off the side of the pool into Alex's arms. 'Well done, George.' He scooped him up onto his hip with one arm and felt a surge of joy as his arms wrapped around his neck. 'That was so much fun.'

Beatrice was waiting with a towel to drop over George's shoulders as they climbed out of the pool, hand in hand.

Her smile was warm and wide. 'Great swimming, George. You're turning into a fish.'

George looked thoughtful. 'What sort?'

'Oh, a dolphin, I think.'

He grinned. 'I like dolphins.'

Beatrice watched George run towards the gate and then turned her gaze back towards Alex. 'It was worth persevering. Learning to trust you will really help his confidence. He'll need that when I…' She looked away, picking up her towel.

'Do I get a towel? Or any praise?'

'Your towel is on that sunbed. And praise might turn your head.'

'I think,' he said softly, securing his towel

around his waist, 'that my head has already been turned.'

'Alex...we agreed that it...this...whatever it is...'

'Is wrong. Yes, I know we did. But wrong feels like it would be more fun than right.'

'Don't. Please don't.' She sucked in a shaky breath and avoided his eyes, looking over at George, who waited, jumping up and down, at the gate.

'At least have dinner with me. We'll be on opposite sides of the table. The staff will be attentive. Nothing will happen.'

'Then why...?'

His smile was slow, lifting one corner of his curved mouth, crinkling the corners of his fathomless, deep green eyes. 'Does there have to be a reason?'

'There probably should be. Otherwise...'

'As it happens, there is. It's my father's birthday next week. In a moment of extreme weakness, I agreed to take George to his party. It seems my parents want to introduce him to some of their friends.'

'That's very good news. It'll be exciting for George...'

She broke off, considering how comfortable George would feel about the plan. He was so accustomed to life at the Villa Eirini that the idea of a change might be intimidating for him.

'Do you think so? I think he might find it frightening. That's why I'd like you to come with us.'

'I don't…' She stopped, shocked, then tried again. 'No, I don't think I can do that. Your parents won't want a stranger at their party. And an employee.'

'You see, that's why I'd like you to have dinner with me. I need an opportunity to persuade you to change your mind.'

CHAPTER THIRTEEN

'IS HE ASLEEP?'

'Shh.' Beatrice put a finger to her lips. 'Only just.'

Stress radiated off Alex in waves. She'd felt it as soon as he entered the dim bedroom where she'd put George to bed. As she watched, he yanked off his tie and undid the top buttons of his shirt. He'd removed his jacket hours ago.

'That was…' Then he shrugged. 'That was no different from usual, except that George was handed round like a prize exhibit at a show of curiosities. I should never have agreed to bring him.'

He dipped his head and the desire to reach out and smooth the lines of tension away from his forehead was strong enough to make Beatrice grip her hands together in front of her.

'Shh,' she repeated, mentally directing the soothing sound towards Alex rather than the sleeping George. 'Come.' She stepped past him, into the adjoining bedroom, which had been allocated to her. 'And for the record, I don't agree.

George coped brilliantly with all the attention. The experience will have been good for him.' She pulled the door between the two bedrooms closed. 'You can relax now.'

'I can never relax under this roof. As soon as you and George left the party, my mother moved up several gears, into super-matchmaking mode.'

In spite of her determination to remain cool and professional, Beatrice's eyes snapped to his face. 'Is that a habit of hers?'

'Yes. She introduced me to the wealthy parents of at least three women she would consider suitable daughters-in-law. In her eyes, I'll only be successful and socially acceptable when I've married someone of whose financial and social position she approves. The former needs to be unassailable and the latter unimpeachable.' Alex paced to the window and leaned his forearm on the glass, resting his forehead on his arm. 'I've told her I'm not interested, countless times.' He pushed himself away from the window and turned to face her. 'But she's never listened to me. Not ever.'

'Well.' Beatrice chose her words carefully. 'Perhaps you *should* listen. A…wife would be good to come home to. A mother for George…'

His eyes narrowed to glittering shards of deep green. 'Seriously? Come on, Beatrice, do you honestly believe that? A society wife, who plays tennis three times a week, flies to Paris to have her hair cut, to Rome to buy her shoes…' He held up his hands, ticking items off his fingers. 'To London…'

Beatrice shook her head, suppressing a smile. 'Stop, Alex. They can't all be like that.'

'What sort of mother to George would one of them make?' he continued, regardless. 'Convince me, and I might reconsider.'

'Is seeing your parents always so stressful?' she asked quietly.

His eyes found hers, and stilled. Their expression held some intense purpose that she didn't understand. His chest heaved. Then he put a hand on her arm and shook his head.

'I need to escape, for a while. Come with me. Please.'

'George…'

'I'll ask my parents to check on him. It'll give them the chance to practice being grandparents and since he's asleep they won't actually have to *do* anything.'

'I'm not sure I should do this, Alex.'

He stopped halfway across the room, his back to her. 'Please,' she heard him say, again.

'Where are we going?'

'To my penthouse.' He pulled into the traffic outside his parents' luxury apartment building and accelerated, overtaking a line of slower cars, the roar and power of the Porsche's engine hitting him between the shoulder blades.

'Is that where you normally go for fresh air?'

He glanced sideways at Beatrice. She sat upright in the passenger seat, her arms folded.

'No. Not usually.'

He drove into the underground car park beneath the apartment block that he owned, parked in his reserved place alongside the elevator, and climbed out, sprinting around to the passenger side to help Beatrice.

She stood with her back against the elevator wall during the swift ride to the top of the building and when he ushered her into his penthouse he watched for her reaction. But she held herself stiffly, and although her eyes widened slightly as she took in her surroundings, she kept silent.

'Wait here.'

He changed quickly into his motorcycle leathers and then carried another set to the living area. Beatrice stood where he'd left her. Her mouth dropped open as she took in his appearance.

'Put these on. They're my sister's, and they'll fit you.'

'Alex, I've never been on a motorbike and I'm not keen to break the habit.'

'Believe me, Beatrice, you'll love it.' He indicated a restroom off the hall. 'You can change in there. Speed is the one addiction I've never been able to give up. We're going for a ride.'

Back in the car park, he handed her a helmet,

then flung a leg across the saddle of his black-and-silver Ducatti.

He had to keep the momentum going. Seeing her walk towards him, hips swaying in the tight-fitting leathers, her hair loose around her shoulders, had almost made him forget to breathe. He'd hustled her into the elevator before he could stop to imagine just how sensual it would be to peel the suit off her, revealing the body he knew to be hidden beneath it, inch by tantalising inch.

Then he'd had to count backwards from one hundred on the journey to the basement car park, and keep his eyes fixed on the numbers unwinding on the display above his head.

Now he turned to look at her. 'Put your hands on my shoulders to climb on and then hold me around the waist.' He started the engine, the initial crescendo of sound settling into a powerful throb between his thighs. 'Tight.'

Carrying a passenger had never felt so good. Her arms wound around his waist. He could feel her knees bracketing his thighs. Best of all, her body moulded itself to his back. Her curves fitted the shape of him, as he'd instinctively known they would. The knowledge that all that separated them were two layers of supple leather turned him on, almost unbearably.

He took the scenic coastal road. It meant a longer ride, and there was still enough light in the sky to admire the spectacular views. As the road unspooled ahead of them and he eased open the throttle he felt Beatrice's arms tighten around his waist and her knees tense against his hips, but as the bike swooped through bends, up and down hills, eating up the miles, she relaxed a little, her body beginning to lean into the corners with his.

The knot of stress beneath his ribs softened and began to unravel.

He wished he could see whether she was smiling, or not. Or whether her eyes were wide open behind the visor or tightly shut. He planned to ask her, later.

Beatrice heard the gear change and sensed that they were slowing down. When they came to a stop, she carried on hugging Alex's waist, waiting for a signal from him. He put his booted feet to the ground and removed his gloves, and then one of his hands covered hers, gently peeling her fingers away from his body. She eased herself upright and pulled off the helmet, shook her hair free and slid off the bike. He quickly followed, putting an arm around her shoulders.

'Just in case you feel wobbly,' he said. 'It's not unusual, if you haven't ridden before.'

Her legs felt shaky and without thinking she leaned against him, her back to his solid chest.

Then she took in their surroundings. The ruins of the ancient temple of Poseidon, god of the sea, loomed above them, the towering rows of columns silhouetted against the evening sky.

'You've brought me to Cape Sounion,' she whispered, turning her head to look up at Alex.

He nodded, his cheek against her hair. 'Mm. Did you enjoy the ride?'

'Yes. Once I accepted there was no escape, I relaxed. It was exhilarating and beautiful.'

His arms tightened across her ribcage, settling her more firmly against the hard planes of his body.

'*This* is beautiful.'

'It's breathtaking. The temple is spectacular. It's as though it's lit from behind.'

'I wasn't only referring to the temple, sweetheart,' he murmured. 'But watch, and you'll see that it is.'

'What do you mean?'

'Shh. Just watch.'

The endearment settled in her heart, even though she tried to bat it away as something casual and meaningless. Myth and romance surrounded them—terms of endearment were practically a requirement. She tipped her head back to rest against his shoulder.

A bright rim of light appeared behind the columns, at their bases, growing in intensity and gaining shape with every second. Beatice held her breath, scarcely able to believe what she was witnessing.

'It's the full moon,' she whispered.

She felt his voice rumble in his chest. 'The Strawberry Moon.'

As she watched, the moon seemed to break free from its tethers. It floated free of the sea and then of the temple, sailing into the indigo sky, laying down a silver pathway across the dark water, all the way to the horizon.

'I don't think I've ever seen anything more ethereal, or beautiful.' She turned in his arms to look up at him. 'I feel as if I've been transported back into the ancient world of the Greek deities.'

His eyes were black in the growing dusk, the muscles of his jaw hard. 'You, Beatrice, are more beautiful than the moon, all the stars and the sun. You would outshine every goddess.' He raised a hand to brush her hair from her face and then cupped her cheek. 'I simply cannot resist the brightness of your flame. Nothing—no-one—has ever set my soul alight as you do.'

He studied her face, taking his time. The guilt about George's birth, the moral correctness of keeping his vow to Enzo and the fact that she was his employee—nothing could stem the tide of molten heat that invaded every muscle and nerve of his body. This time, there would be no stopping their kiss.

Her eyes, slate-grey in the dusk, were wide, and fixed on his, reflecting a kind of wonderment. Her lips, about which he'd fantasised, day and night, since he'd first seen her, were parted a little. His own eyelids fluttered closed for a few unbearable seconds as the tip of her tongue touched the little indentation in her top lip.

'Alex?' It was a whispered sound on the light breeze that played with the ends of her hair.

'Yes.' Hundreds of words crowded his brain—all the things he wanted to say to her, all the ways he wanted to tell her how he felt. None of them would do. He cupped her face with his hands, brushing her temples with his fingers, gently angling her head.

When their lips touched it was featherlight. He drew back a fraction, checking that she was alright. Her hands moved from his chest, over his shoulders, to tangle in his hair, pulling him down towards her.

That was when his tightly wound control snapped and he spun free, all the reasons not to do this vaporising. His mouth landed on hers, taking everything she could give, wanting more. The voice in his head telling him to stop was drowned out by the rush of blood through his veins and the hammering of his heart. A louder voice told him stopping was impossible.

Her lips were as soft as he'd imagined, and she tasted of roses and cinnamon and pure longing. He nipped her bottom lip lightly and she gasped, opening her mouth to allow his tongue to invade her sweetness and slide against hers. He cupped the back of her head in his hand while the other found its way down the line of her spine, to splay across the small of her back, trapping her against him.

The leather between them drove him wild and he groaned into her mouth, desperate to be closer to her. Need raged through him, leaving no room for doubt that this was what they should be doing.

When they broke apart, their breathing mingling in ragged gasps, he held her as if he could never let her go, cradling her cheek against his chest, catching a tear that trickled down her cheek with a finger.

'You're crying.' He stroked a hand over her head and threaded his fingers through the length of her hair. 'I'm sorry. I didn't mean to upset you.'

She shook her head. 'You didn't. It's just that kissing you, at last, is such a relief. I've longed for it, but we said—we know—that it's wrong. We shouldn't have let this happen, but I just want more. I want you to undo me, and I want to feel you come undone in my arms. I don't want this to be wrong.'

He tightened his hold on her, rocking her back and forth. 'How can something be wrong, when it feels so right?'

'I…don't know. I don't understand these feelings. They've overwhelmed me and I can't fight them, anymore. I don't want to.'

Alex pressed a hard, open-mouth kiss to her temple. 'Come.' He gripped one of her hands in his and led her back to the bike. 'We're going home.'

CHAPTER FOURTEEN

THEY KISSED AGAIN as they waited for the elevator in the underground garage.

The ride back had been tortuous. Every nerve ending on her skin seemed to be crying out to be touched, caressed, released from this unbearable anticipation. When they stumbled into the elevator he walked her to the back wall, pushing a knee between her thighs and then lifting her so that her ankles locked behind him, kissing her so hard she struggled to breathe.

She hardly noticed the spectacular view of the floodlit Parthenon, framed in the vast windows of Alex's penthouse, as he carried her into the open-plan living area and let her slide slowly down his body, steadying her as her feet touched the floor.

Her hands gripped his shoulders, but he closed them in his, drawing them down to cage them against his chest and beneath its fevered rise and fall she could feel the thunder of his heartbeat between them.

'Beatrice.' Her name on his lips felt like a benediction, and she closed her eyes, absorbing it. 'Are you sure? Because if you're not…' He took a sharp breath. 'Please say no now, and we'll stop…but I don't know how much longer—'

'I'm sure.' Her voice sounded alien to her own ears. 'I…don't want to stop. I'm a little afraid that I'll…that you'll be disappointed…but I'm sure.'

Concern and compassion drew his brows together and he shook his head. 'Don't be afraid. Don't ever be afraid. Not of me.'

His mouth became gentle, his lips moving with slow insistence over hers, sweeping her away to where nothing existed but the two of them and the exquisite feelings radiating from her core to the tips of her fingers and toes. But when he reached for the zipper at her neck and began to slide it down, towards her waist, her deep breaths turned choppy and uneven.

Still kissing her, his hands eased the soft leather over her shoulders and down her arms, pulling her hands out of the sleeves. Cool air brushed her skin as she stood in the circle of his arms in her underwear and the camisole she'd kept on under the suit.

She wanted to cross her arms over her chest to hide from him, but he broke the kiss and caught her hands in his.

'So beautiful,' he whispered, reverence sliding through his voice. He dipped his head and placed his mouth on the hollow between her collarbones.

'I've wanted to taste you here, ever since…' His tongue touched her skin and she gasped. 'Ever since the first moment I saw you, sitting in the courtyard of the Villa Eirini,' he murmured, 'when you were still Bea Antonini, and a strait-laced governess.'

'You wanted to kiss a strait-laced governess?' Her voice felt impeded.

'Mm. Somehow, I knew that beneath that sober exterior, lay something sensual and sexy and…'

The jarring ringtone of his mobile phone pierced the air.

'Your phone, Alex.' Confusion swamped her. Real-life intruding on their intimacy felt brutal and jarring.

He swore. 'I'll ignore it. Don't move away from me.' He pulled her back against him, but she could hear the stress in his voice.

'But what if it's important? What if George…?'

He held her, his hands pushing between the leather suit and her ribs. The phone stopped ringing but immediately started again.

'It can't be about George. He's safely asleep…'

'Alex, please. Answer it.'

He pulled the phone roughly from a pocket at the side of his suit and turned away from her, punching at the screen.

When he turned back to her, every trace of colour had drained from his face.

'It's my father. George fell and banged his head.

He's at the hospital, and he's asking for you.' She stood, frozen in shock, but Alex put his hands on her shoulders and turned her around, urging her towards the powder room door, the palm of his hand in the small of her back. 'We must get to the hospital.'

Beatrice fumbled with the leather bike suit, her shaking fingers unable to grip it. She couldn't ask Alex for help. Not now.

Guilt and shock churned in her stomach, making her feel nauseated. They'd been kissing, their thoughts only for each other and for how they could get back to the penthouse and rip each other's clothes off, and George had woken, confused and frightened, and fallen and banged his head on the marble stairs.

What if he'd been concussed? Had a brain injury? How could she ever live with the consequences of their selfish behaviour?

'Beatrice? We need to hurry.' Alex's voice, tight with anxiety, was outside the door.

'I—I know. But I can't…' Her voice broke on a sob and the door was pulled open.

Alex was pale as parchment, lines of anxiety etched on his face.

'Let me help you.' He gripped the suit at the waist and peeled it down over her hips and legs. There was no hint of desire left in his touch or his voice. His movements were efficient and quick, lifting her feet and freeing her from the clinging suit. Then he handed her the dress she'd worn to the party. 'I'll wait at the elevator.' He glanced at his watch.

They drove to the hospital in tense silence. Beatrice watched the muscles of his thigh flexing with his need to floor the accelerator. He swore as yet another set of traffic lights turned to red.

They were led through the bright lights of the emergency department and then through double doors into a ward.

George looked small and fragile, lying in the hospital bed. His eyes were open, watching the door, and when he saw his father and Beatrice he tried to sit up. The nurse at his side laid a hand on his shoulder and spoke to him quietly and he subsided against the pillows.

'Beetriss.' Tears flooded his blue eyes and spilled down his cheeks. 'I was lost and I hurt my head.'

She folded him in her arms, overwhelmed with relief. He was conscious and he recognised her. 'I'm so sorry, George. We'll get you home as soon as possible.'

Nicholas, Alex's father, rose from a chair and she saw Alex turn on him.

'What happened?' His voice was a furious whisper. 'You were supposed to check on him.'

The older man shrugged. 'I asked Helena, but she forgot.'

'*Forgot?* And you call *me* irresponsible.'

His father was at the door. 'I noted that it was Beatrice he asked for. What sort of father does that make you?'

The door closed behind him and her eyes met Alex's. He looked exhausted and stressed, but most of all he looked angry, and she was afraid that anger was directed not only at his father, but at her, too.

The doctors assured Alex that the bump on George's head would subside and he'd suffered no more serious injuries, and discharged him the following morning. Alex drove them to the airport.

Grim-faced and monosyllabic, he carried George onto his jet. Beatrice kept her face averted from him, in the car and on the aircraft, afraid of the blame she might see in his eyes.

After his supper Alex picked George up and took him to his bedroom. Since arriving at the hospital the previous evening he had barely let him out of his sight. Each time he'd carried him, George had clung to him and when they'd boarded the plane Alex had had to prise his arms from around his neck to strap him safely into his seat. If there was anything positive to take from this it was that Alex and George had formed a stronger bond.

Back in the sanctuary of her suite, Beatrice showered, slipped into her belted robe and sat at her open window. The peaceful view usually soothed her, but now the memory of Alex's shuttered face intruded on her thoughts.

Perhaps he was angry because George had grown too close to her and she resolved to create more distance between them.

A soft knock on the door surprised her.

Alex still wore the faded jeans and rumpled shirt he'd dressed in yesterday evening in their rush to reach the hospital. Stress still lined his face, but his eyes were softer, some of the anger gone from their dark olive depths. He still hadn't shaved and his palm rasped across his rough jaw.

If she was about to feel the sharp edge of his temper, she had no defence to offer. Her priority should have been George's well-being. Nothing should have made her lose sight of that. *Nothing.*

She folded her arms and took a step back from him.

'Beatrice.'

Her heart flipped, but she pressed her arms against her ribcage and pressed her lips together.

'I'm sorry,' he said softly.

'You're *sorry*? I—I thought you were angry.'

'I am angry, but not with you. With myself. And I'm sorry I've been offhand with you. It was… I haven't known how to be. I was so anxious, yet still on a high after we… I had to hold myself together, until he went to sleep.'

'Perhaps you *should* be angry with me, Alex. I should never have left George in a strange house with people he didn't know. I could have predicted that he'd wake and be confused and upset. He'd been excited and hyped up.'

He shook his head and looked past her, out towards the sea. 'He's my son and *I* shouldn't have left him, either. I didn't give you any option. I put you under pressure. I had to get away from that party, from all that…*expectation*…and I wanted… I *needed* you with me. I should have been able to put myself second, for once.'

'I wanted to go with you, so much.'

'When I heard my father's voice it felt as if the whole world had stopped. Knowing he'd asked for you, and not for me…'

'I'm so sorry. You must be so hurt. We'll change things…'

'No. Don't apologise. *Of course* he'd ask for you. He's grown to love and trust you. You've made his life fun and exciting. You're always there for him. He's only just beginning to realise that he can enjoy being with me, too, and that's all thanks to you.'

'You should be the most important, constant presence in George's life. I won't always be here, but you will be.'

'Won't you? Have you even considered the options?'

'I love my job in Geneva, Alex.'

'But you love it here. Don't you?'

She dropped her head. 'Yes. I do. But you'll

have to consider George's future. In a year or two he should go to school. He needs friends his own age and to fit into a classroom situation. Keeping him isolated on Ithaca has been good for him while he adjusted to his new circumstances, but it won't equip him for life in the real world.'

'I only want the best for him. Keeping that in mind helps in some way to assuage the guilt I feel about his mother.'

'You're doing a great job, Alex. What happened wasn't your fault. But you do need to think about the future.'

The thought of leaving the Villa Eirini made her stomach clench and her heart hurt. She couldn't tell Alex that the reason she couldn't stay, beyond the summer, was him. He *knew* her. Not just who she was, on the surface, but how all her pieces fitted together. Some of those pieces were misshapen by the grief she carried, and he was okay with that. She didn't have to pretend to be anyone, or anything, else.

How heartbreaking that the one person who saw her for herself would never commit to her. Although he loved George, and was learning to show it, a relationship and fatherhood had never been part of his plan. Nothing would change that.

'Beatrice? Last night—'

She turned her face away. 'Last night…the bike ride, the temple in the moonlight…you. It was…magical.'

'I needed you, and you...'

'I needed you, too. I *wanted* you. But although I regret George's accident, perhaps it was a timely interruption.'

'Do you...regret...what happened between us?' The catch in his voice betrayed how difficult the question was for him.

'No. I don't. It shouldn't have happened, but how could I ever regret something so beautiful?'

If he wanted to take her in his arms again, she knew she wouldn't have the strength to resist him. Her blood roared in her ears and her throat ached with emotion. But he just nodded once, swung on his heel and left the room.

Only when she exhaled did she realise that she'd been holding her breath.

CHAPTER FIFTEEN

HE HAD NO idea how many laps he'd swum. Any hope that his overworked mind would eventually move into a zone where he wasn't thinking about Beatrice had been lost within the first five minutes. The memories of what had happened between them three nights before played on repeat in his brain and showed no sign of slowing or stopping.

Beatrice updated him on George's progress regularly, discussing plans for the days ahead. She'd adopted a manner of cool detachment, which he wished he could emulate.

After an initial quiet day, making sure that there'd been no further ill effects from the accident, he'd taken George swimming again.

And yesterday they'd gone to the café on the beach, without Beatrice, for strawberry ice creams. Would he spend the rest of his life comparing the taste of her mouth with every other sweet treat in the world, and finding them all lacking?

She said she didn't regret it. But she maintained that his father's phone call had been timely, that it shouldn't have happened. Until he'd untangled his feelings he couldn't ask her what she meant, but it seemed she felt she'd been stopped from doing something she *would* regret.

Her scent seemed to linger everywhere. The sound of her voice followed him to his study. Over and over, he imagined himself back in the penthouse, his hands on Beatrice's ribs, the leather suit folded to her waist, and then the ringtone of his phone.

Perhaps it was the interruption he'd needed, too, because it had saved him from breaking his vow to Enzo. Should he be grateful, or was the vow, with one half of it broken, now worth nothing at all?

Hookups and sex had always been easy for him. Was this simply unrequited lust? He hated that he'd even allowed that thought to form. Beatrice was so different from any other woman he'd known. She deserved the fulfilment she gained from teaching, and a partner who would cherish her for her qualities of empathy and honesty. Someone who would give her the children he was sure she wanted and who would love her for herself, not for her name or fortune.

If such a thing as love existed.

She most definitely did not deserve a man like him.

All his distraction techniques, and he knew a few, failed.

Pounding the treadmill, beating the hell out of the punch bag and lifting insane weights hadn't touched his frustration. He had no further weapons to test if swimming didn't work.

It was driving him crazy.

He sprinted a final length of the pool, then surged out of the water, resting his folded arms on the side, his chest heaving, and wiped the water from his face.

'Alex.'

It felt as if his heart stopped, then resumed beating more quickly than his sprint merited. He inched his head around, afraid any quick movement would shatter the moment and catapult him back into reality.

But here Beatrice was, not a figment of his wishful imagination, but sitting with her feet in the water, her hands beside her hips. Her pink bikini was a soft shade of violet in the semi-darkness.

'I thought…' He slid back into the water. 'I'm sorry. I didn't know you were planning to swim. I'll go and take a shower. I'm sorry.'

'Alex,' she repeated. 'Stop apologising. I came to find you.'

His brain, which had been thinking of all the things he wanted to say to her, froze. All he could think of was how beautiful she looked, with her hair tied back, wayward tendrils framing her face, her elegant neck, long, lean limbs that gleamed in the dusk, and her body… He swallowed hard.

The perfect globes of her breasts, captured in the triangles of her bikini top, and the rounded curves of her hips sent heat licking through him. It ignited with a slow white-hot flame in his belly and he knew only one way to douse it. That wasn't going to happen, not now, never, with Beatrice.

She'd wanted him, as much as he'd wanted her, but there could be no going back to where they'd been, under the moon at Cape Sounion or in his dark penthouse, with the floodlit Parthenon as their witness.

Finally, he found one rasping word.

'Why?'

Beatrice's answer was to slip into the pool beside him. The water was warm, but she still gasped softly as it closed around her body. She held on to the side with one hand, her other hand and legs moving languidly, keeping her afloat.

A foot brushed Alex's thigh and he jerked away, shocked by the shaft of sensation that pierced him. Her free hand came to rest on his shoulder, and he tensed his muscles, trying to resist his reaction.

'Because there is something unfinished between us.'

Three nights ago they'd shared a wild embrace. They'd almost been skin to skin. His hands had been on her ribcage, he'd felt her breasts pressing against his chest, and their kisses had been deep—*so deep.*

Now he had to keep a distance between them.

To cross it would be to go against what she wanted. She was glad they'd been forced to stop. She would have regretted going any further.

He tried to move away, but her fingers tightened.

'You didn't want to finish it.' He felt a tremor shake her. 'You were glad we were interrupted…'

'I said the interruption was timely, and it was, because it gave me time to think about what I want.'

'I can't give you what you want, Beatrice.'

'You don't know what I want.'

'Okay, well what you deserve, then, which is someone who will give you all the normal things. A home, children and love, if you believe in it. I can't imagine my life without George, but I will never be able to commit to anyone else.'

'I will want those things one day, when I return to my other life, but that day isn't today. What we share feels otherworldly to me. This place, the beauty of the Villa Eirini, the timelessness of Ithaca are special, sealed off from the real world. To leave may break my heart, but it will mend, and I'll always have this.'

'Beatrice…'

She shook her head. 'Let me finish. I want to make this complete, the memories perfect. I know it means breaking the promise you made to Enzo, and if you cannot do that I'll understand. You asked before if I was sure, and I am sure—' she slipped her hand around his neck to cup the back of his head, drawing him towards her '—that I want you.'

Alex felt as if tight bands restricting his body were being slowly removed. His breathing deepened, his limbs, aching and tense from swimming, relaxed.

There was no urgency this time, just hours and days stretching ahead of them. He took her hand and swam with her to a place where they could both stand in the water, then ran his hands over her shoulders and down her arms, interlacing his fingers with hers. Their eyes locked; he tugged her towards him. When their lips met it felt achingly familiar yet almost unbearably exciting and new.

She murmured something and he raised his head a little. 'Are you okay?'

'Mm. Just…so good. I feel like a spring inside me is unwinding.'

He smiled against her temple, but his next kiss was harder, more insistent, and she responded with a slide of her tongue along his, her fingers digging into his shoulders.

With a muttered '*yes*' he slipped an arm around her, the other behind her knees, swept her out of the water and strode up the steps.

He lowered her to the ground, reached for the towel from the sunbed and wrapped it around her shoulders. Hugging her to his side, they walked towards the gate.

Beatrice hesitated. 'What if someone sees us? The staff…'

His mouth found hers again, kissing her hard, while his fingers speared her hair, his thumbs on her jaw. 'We'll go up the secret staircase,' he breathed, when he broke the kiss. 'No one will see us.'

They climbed through the terraced gardens, stopping twice more, overcome by the need for another embrace, another fevered kiss. Alex led her along a hidden path through a grove of lemon trees, which emerged at a place where the shrubbery almost touched the villa. Keeping her clamped against him, he pushed aside the rampant honeysuckle that grew up the old walls to reveal an ancient wooden door with a keypad set into it. He punched in numbers and shouldered the door open.

A staircase wound upwards. The sounds of their breathing was loud in the dark, narrow space, but the door at the top opened into a dimly lit, austere bedroom.

He watched Beatrice take in the pale grey walls, the polished wooden floor and his wide bed covered with a grey linen throw. The room was starkly modern and minimalist compared with the decoration of the rest of the mansion.

The door clicked shut behind them and Alex

slid the towel from around her shoulders. He studied her for long seconds, the sudden apprehension in her dark eyes making his heart clench.

'Come.' He lifted her again and covered the distance to the bed in three strides. He lowered her onto it, then stretched out next to her, studying every detail of her, pushing back her hair, then planting quick kisses on her forehead, along her jaw, down the side of her neck.

He paused at the hollow between her collarbones, remembering her previous response when he'd kissed her there, gratified when she repeated it, with greater intensity.

He raised his head, watching the quickening of her breath and how her dilating pupils darkened her eyes.

'Alex…' Her hands gripped his shoulders, and he dropped his head again, kissing a path down to the edge of her bikini top. His fingers found her cheek, his thumb her bottom lip, and she drew it into the soft moistness of her mouth.

'Beatrice.' The sound was harsh.

Ripples of sensation began to build in him, unstoppable.

Reaching to the tie at the back of her neck, he took a deep, shaky breath.

'Do you still want me to undo you?'

She smiled a little and their eyes locked. 'I do.'

He'd been wrong about the lack of urgency. A wave of sensation engulfed him, and he took her with him, clinging to him, crying out and begging for release, but before his body took over, utterly, he reached for the drawer in the nightstand. ‘No,’ she murmured, ‘don’t leave me…’

‘Shh. I’m not leaving you, but we need this, sweetheart.’

He gathered her into his arms again, stroking her hair from her face, tucking a strand behind her ear, the skin of her temple silky under his mouth. He brushed his thumbs across her cheeks, finding her lips with his. The way she moved beneath him stoked the fire burning low in his abdomen and although he tried to hold back, the heat of it grew and built until it overwhelmed him. As it consumed them both he heard the beat of his name on her lips, and his own guttural shout.

Afterwards, he held her, her face buried in his shoulder, their breathing heavy and deep. ‘I’m sorry. I wanted to be gentle, but…’

‘I wanted to feel you come undone in my arms. Remember?’

‘Yes. But I think I hurt you. And… I thought you’d be more experienced. You’re so beautiful. So desirable. I didn’t give you time.’

She went still, then tipped her head back, her eyes searching his face. ‘Do you think I’m… cold?’

The doubt in her eyes touched something deep inside him and he pulled her roughly against his chest, claiming another deep kiss, one hand cupping the back of her head, the other gripping her hip.

'*Cold?*' He shook his head. 'The way you move—the way you…*give*. The sounds you make. How could I think you're cold?'

'Just something someone once said.' Her fingertips trailed down his spine, her palms coming to rest in the small of his back. He shifted against her, loving how the movement made her lips part in a soft gasp. 'It was the only other time.'

'Tell me his name, and I'll…'

'It doesn't matter. I know now why I've waited.' She pressed her mouth to his chest. 'It was worth the wait. I never knew I could feel like that. Are you still planning to take a shower?'

'Mm. Perhaps a cold one.'

'Let's make it a hot one.'

As the water cascaded over them, Beatrice reached up. 'I've wanted to massage these muscles since the first time I saw you. Turn around.'

She dug her fingers into the knots under his skin, and he groaned, resting his forehead against the shower wall. When he could bear it no longer, he turned, lifting her so that her legs wound around his waist, supporting her back against the tiles.

'Can I ask you something?'

'If you're quick.' He tipped her chin up and kissed the base of her throat. 'Because any moment now my brain is going to cease to function in a rational way.'

She plunged her fingers into his hair, scraping her nails against his scalp. 'Why is there a secret stairway to your room?'

'So that…' He had to breathe as she leaned into him. 'So that the master of the house could… smuggle his mistress into his bedroom.'

She drew back. 'Does that make me your mistress?'

'No.' He pulled her against him again, sliding a hand between them. 'It makes you my lover.'

CHAPTER SIXTEEN

EACH DAY BEATRICE devised an activity that would help to build the relationship between George and his father.

He read the story of Odysseus to George again and took him to the site of the ancient palace, where Penelope, bound by love and loyalty, had waited twenty years for the return of her beloved husband from the Trojan Wars.

They swam in the sea and sailed on a yacht.

Although Beatrice celebrated the strengthening relationship between father and son, silently her heart ached. What she was doing was right for George and Alex, but at the same time she was paving the way to leaving Ithaca at the end of the summer.

She'd never regret a moment of this time. The memories would be locked into her heart, her feelings kept secret. She would never, ever tell Alex about her feelings for him.

They met each evening, sometimes for dinner on the terrace and a walk in the gardens before slipping up the secret staircase to Alex's rooms. On other evenings he came quietly to her suite. They swam after dark and made love in the moon-lit pool. Once, they took a picnic onto the *Penelope* and lay together on the deep cushions, watching the stars sway above them with the gentle rocking of the launch.

Being kissed awake as dawn softened the night sky became Beatrice's favourite way to start the day. Alex's stubbled jaw would scrape against her cheek, his warm mouth would find hers, and they'd make love again, languorously exploring every inch of each other's bodies.

With every day and night, leaving him felt more impossible, and more necessary. Sometimes she knew that if he asked her to stay, on any terms, she'd agree. Other times, she vowed to cling to her own sense of self and stand by her decision, because one day, he would tire of her and want to return to his old life. She could not drift, waiting for that to happen. It would break her heart and her spirit to feel him lose interest in her and look for fulfilment elsewhere.

They'd been lovers for three weeks, and the temperature had continued to climb. They lay in Alex's bed, under a linen sheet, their bodies slick and sensitised. Beatrice rested her head on his chest and spread her fingers across his abdomen.

'Enzo called me this afternoon.' She felt his

stomach muscles tense under her fingers and his arm around her shoulders tighten. His shoulder blades shifted against the pillows. She glanced up at him, seeing his jaw flex.

'Why are you telling me?' Stress sharpened his voice. 'This is our time. Don't spoil it.'

She stroked her fingers through the soft hair that arrowed down his stomach, and he wrapped his fingers around her wrist, his breath hissing. 'Because what he said concerns you.'

He moved her hand from his stomach but kept hold of her wrist. 'You *took* his call?'

She nodded, her cheek rubbing against his chest. 'Yes, I did.'

'Why?'

She sighed. 'I almost didn't. But he's my brother—my only family—and whatever has happened between him and me, and you, I miss him, and I need him.'

'You *need* him?' He let go of her hand and pushed himself upright, frowning down at her. 'What do you need him for? Don't I care for you enough?'

'Oh, Alex, of course you do. You're everything…' She stopped, biting her lip. 'He wants to put things right between us. He…understands how much he hurt me, and you.'

'He broke a promise to me.'

Beatrice pulled up her knees. 'And this?' She swept out an arm to encompass the two of them, the rumpled bed, lifting her eyebrows at him. 'This is not a broken promise, too?'

'He *married* my sister.'

She'd never imagined she could feel anger towards him, but it hit her now and she twisted around to face him. 'So that makes it different? Because you have no intention of marrying me, this doesn't count as a broken promise?'

'I have no intention of marrying anyone. Enzo didn't, either. We were always clear about that.'

It was what she'd always known but hearing him say it drove something sharp between her ribs, and she hugged her knees to her chest.

'Have you considered,' she said, her eyes fixed on her knees, 'that they might have fallen in love?'

'*Love.*' In a swift movement, Alex pushed the sheet aside and swung his legs off the bed. 'Do you think he loves my sister?'

Beatrice couldn't bear to look at him, but she could feel the waves of fury coming off him. She dropped her forehead to her knees. 'Yes.' Her voice was muffled. 'I think he does.'

'How do you believe that makes me feel? I know what he's like. I know all the things he did. *All* of them. He left a trail of broken hearts behind him, longer than Casanova's. What if my sister is his next victim?'

She lifted her head. 'That's interesting, Alex.' Her voice shook. 'Because that's what he told me about you. He said you were "mad, bad and dangerous to know." Why do you think I wanted to work for *you*? I knew how angry it would make him. I wanted to show him I could take care of myself.'

'There's a difference between us, though, Beatrice. I never promised a second date. I never swapped phone numbers. I never broke a heart. Yes, I've broken my promise, too, and I feel guilty as all hell, and ashamed of my weakness, but this—' he gestured between them '—is going to end, soon, because you're going to leave, and it won't be messy. Not like it'll be when Enzo walks out on my sister because someone else has caught his eye.'

She scrambled up, flinging the tangled linen aside, fury driving her from the bed. 'My brother will never do that. He loves her, and I can understand how it happened. If you'd been more accessible, they'd have told you how they felt, but they knew how difficult life was for you, with George, and they didn't want to add to your stress. Maybe it was a misjudgement, but they want to put it right…'

She stood in front of him, shaking, tears threatening to turn her into a sobbing, quivering mess.

'Did he say *how* they plan to put it right?' His voice, which usually spoke to her with such gentle tenderness, sounded cold as ice.

She took a deep, gulping breath. 'They're having a party, in two weeks' time, for all the family and friends they didn't invite to their wedding. They want us to go.'

His eyes narrowed, glittering and dark. '*Us?* You told him about *us*?'

'Yes…*no*…that is, I told him I was here, and I told him how it had come about. He was angry, which was what I'd intended, but he understood why I did it. But *us*…*this*…what we've… I told you I wanted to keep this just for me…for you, too, if you want to remember it. No, I didn't tell him that we're…lovers. It's too…precious. Too… fragile.' Her voice dropped to a whisper. 'To let the outside world in would break it.'

'I think,' he said, his voice flat, 'that we can consider it broken already, Beatrice.' He walked into the bathroom and closed the door and she heard the snick of the catch as he locked it.

Alex had once explained that before he'd modernised the Villa Eirini the ensuite had been a writing room. The solid oak door, like all the others in the house, had been made from wood harvested on the island and was as old as the original structure.

Beatrice stared at it. The passing centuries had left their marks on its surface. Scuffs and scratches had been polished, but each must have told its own story, now long forgotten. The brass handle gleamed with use.

Now she wanted to leave a mark of her own. She wanted to hammer on the door with her fists, drag her nails across its surface and shout at Alex through its solid thickness, telling him she was sorry, asking him to turn the lock, turn time back and take her in his arms again. She'd call Enzo and tell him she could never forgive him, and she wouldn't go to their party.

But she stood in the middle of the room, clenched her fists at her sides and clamped her jaw shut. Alex was being unreasonable. He was employing double standards, and maligning Enzo's character.

While she'd said she wanted to keep their relationship a secret between the two of them, the fact that he would rather lose her than ever consider making it public felt like a knife twisting in her heart.

He regretted breaking his vow; he was ashamed of what they'd done. Ashamed of *her*.

Choking back a sob, she snatched up the cotton tunic she'd been wearing, through which Alex had kissed and stroked her before eventually removing it, his fingers fumbling with haste. She pulled it over her head, gathered up her underwear in hands that shook and slipped out of his room.

Crying was not an option. Beatrice stood under the pulsing spray of the power shower, the needle stinging of the water no distraction from the ache in her heart. She'd chosen this with her eyes wide open, always knowing it would have to end.

She just hadn't anticipated the depth of pain that ending it would inflict.

She would not be crushed by it. She'd prepared George for the fact that she would be leaving. She'd tell Alex she needed to return to Switzerland at once. The thought of staying on Ithaca was unbearable.

And she would go to Enzo and Thaleia's party in Rome. She'd forgive them for excluding her from their wedding and she'd celebrate their future with them. There was no place in her life for regret and bitterness. She'd learned as a child, with the loss of their parents, that self-pity is isolating and sadness only drove people away. Aged eight, she'd made up her mind to celebrate her parents' memory by being happy and positive, even though she was hiding a heart that was broken and afraid of the future.

Tears threatened when she thought of George and how he'd been ripped from his life and dumped in another one, with strangers he didn't understand in a place horribly alien from his home in London. She hoped she'd helped him on his journey of recovery. If Alex and George formed a loving bond this would all have been worthwhile.

Not quite all. There was her fractured heart to consider, but she'd think about that when she was back in the familiar and comforting surroundings of her apartment in Geneva.

Enzo had never sounded happier than when he'd called her that afternoon. Every word he spoke of Thaleia was warmed through with love. He'd been briefly angry and concerned when he heard what Beatrice had done but apologised for making her feel she'd had to do it. If she was safe, he'd said, and staying away from that womaniser Alex, he was happy for her. 'Make sure you lock your door at night!' had been his parting comment.

There was no point in trying to explain any of this to Alex. Love, he implied, was some sort of fabricated fantasy, which would shrivel when exposed to the harsh light of reality.

Honesty was a quality he prized over all others, but she could never tell him the truth, now. Because the truth was that she'd fallen in love with him.

CHAPTER SEVENTEEN

ALTHOUGH HE EXPECTED Beatrice to have left when he emerged from the bathroom, Alex still felt an irrational surge of disappointment when he found the bedroom empty.

He pulled the towel from around his waist and rubbed furiously at his wet hair. The semi-sheer top, which had driven him wild, and her lacy underwear were all gone.

A glance at the bed made his gut twist with pain. The tumbled linen, which they'd both thrown off in anger, the indentations in the soft pillows where their heads had lain close only moments before she'd told him about Enzo's call, the nightstand drawer, which, in his haste, he hadn't closed, all hurt him to look at.

He wished he could smooth it all out, close the drawer, make everything pristine, and start again.

He shook his head and swore. He'd screwed up something that he was now realising, too late, had become very important to him. When he hit a problem in business, he always found a way to overcome it. Everything could be fixed, but not this.

He told himself that a woman becoming important was a *very* bad thing, and he shouldn't want to fix it, but that didn't help. He wanted things to return to how they'd been, just a short while before, but they couldn't.

Not if Beatrice insisted on mending her relationship with Enzo. Not if she insisted on going to their make-up party, which was obviously being planned to smooth all the feathers they'd ruffled in Italian and Greek society by secretly getting married.

Nothing could drag him to the event. Okay, so he'd broken his promise too, and he wasn't proud of that. In fact, if he examined his conscience in greater detail, he was ashamed that he'd been unable to resist Beatrice, but while he regretted his lapse and the evident weakness in his moral fibre, he couldn't regret what had happened between them, no matter how hypocritical that made him.

Because being with her, in her arms, in her bed, had been the most beautiful, transcending thing that had ever happened to him. The depth of the connection he felt to her and the soaring heights of pure ecstasy they'd reached together were different from anything that had gone before.

He ached to feel her lithe body moving against his, her smooth, supple skin like satin under his questing fingers. Even after his shower, the taste of her remained in his mouth and he knew her captivating scent would linger on the sheets and pillows of his bed.

There was no point in trying to sleep. In this room he was surrounded, enveloped by her, even though she'd gone.

Perhaps by the morning she'd have reconsidered and decided to refuse the party invitation, but the certainty that this wouldn't play out like he hoped was a twisting lead weight in his stomach. Beatrice was so honest, so genuine—so *giving*. If she'd told Enzo she'd go to the party, there was no way he could change her mind, especially not for the sake of his pride, his hurt at Enzo and Thaleia's behaviour and his determination to be the good guy in all of this. He'd stopped being the good guy the moment his eyes had first fallen on Beatrice.

He'd given into desire when he should have been strong enough to resist it.

He tried to ignore the clamour of his body, which persisted in telling him that all he really wanted was to be holding Beatrice, skin to skin, her silky hair tumbling over her shoulders and her mouth on his.

This was what came of breaking his cardinal rule of never spending more than one night with a woman. He'd got to know all of her and yet still each time they were together he discovered something new about her. She was like a story that kept unfolding beneath him and he couldn't wait to read the next chapter, every night.

To give it up felt not just difficult, but impossible, like the worst addiction.

At breakfast the following morning, Beatrice felt Maria's eyes on her. She met the older woman's questioning gaze with a shrug. 'I have a headache.' She poured juice into George's cup, 'It'll pass.' She couldn't understand Maria's muttered Greek but the way she banged a saucepan into the sink spoke louder than her words were soft.

She willed the morning away and when she'd settled George with a book for his quiet time, she knocked on Alex's study door.

He turned from the window as she closed the door behind her and walked into the middle of the room.

Twenty-four hours ago, she would have walked into the circle of his arms, and he would have buried his fingers in her hair and kissed her forehead, then worked his way down to her lips. His hands would have smoothed over her back and hips, his fingers would have explored all the places where slight pressure, or a feather-light stroke, would make her gasp and smile against his mouth.

It felt jolting to leave space between them. His face was pale, a frown between his brows and his hair untidy. He wore the clothes he'd discarded on the bedroom floor last night and she suspected that, like herself, he'd spent the hours between then and now awake.

She glanced across at the sofa, looking for signs that he'd slept on it, but all she got was a punch of emotion, remembering how they'd made love on it, more than once.

'I hoped it was you.' His arms were braced at his sides, his shoulders pulled fiercely back.

She closed her eyes briefly, swaying with exhaustion. 'I would like to leave as soon as possible. I understand you'll have to find someone else to care for George. Perhaps Dafni…'

He raised a hand, and she flinched, bracing herself to not give into his touch, but then he dropped it again. 'But the party isn't for another fortnight. Surely you'll stay until then?'

'No.'

'Then I'll care for George myself.'

She shook her head, just wanting this over before she cracked and said she'd stay, on any terms, just for one more night with him. 'I thought your work made that impossible.'

He nodded. 'It makes it difficult, yes. But he'll be…confused. Sad. I'll need to help him cope with what will be another loss.'

'Oh, I…' She dropped her head. 'Thank you. I'll feel…happier…knowing you're taking care of him.'

She heard his rough inhalation.

'That is, of course, if you won't change your mind.'

His words surprised her.

'Would you be prepared to change yours?'

The emotion that flickered in his too-dark eyes was brief, but the way he shut it down delivered a painful twist to her heart.

'You know I won't do that.'

'Can you tell me why? Are you too proud to admit that you're only human, after all? That you couldn't resist the demands of your body and that weakness scares you?'

'What I did was wrong and I regret my lapse, but…'

'It takes two, Alex. It was as much my decision as your lapse that led us to this, and for my part I don't believe it was wrong. It has felt wondrous—something precious that I will cherish. Not something shameful or regrettable.'

He moved back to lean against the desk, gripping its edge between his fingers.

'I didn't say I regret what's happened between us.'

'But you're not prepared to acknowledge it to anyone else. Yes, I'd like to keep these memories safe here with you, but if Enzo or Thaleia asks me, I'll tell them the truth about us. They love each other and they'll understand.'

He pushed himself upright, the lines between his brows deepening, his lips thinning.

'What do you mean?'

Beatrice backed to the door. 'I mean I won't

hide this away like some embarrassing secret. You're sheltering behind your moral rectitude, Alex, because you're afraid of admitting your feelings. You're afraid that if you do, you'll be vulnerable to emotions that frighten you.'

'I keep my emotions under control. They don't scare me.'

'They don't scare you *because* you keep them so firmly pinned down. Courage means facing something that frightens you but doing it anyway. Admitting that you love someone, like Enzo and Thaleia have done, takes strength and bravery.'

'I've never told anyone that I love them because I haven't needed to. And nobody—*nobody*—has ever told me they love me, either. I don't plan—I don't *want*—to change that.'

Beatrice's fingers closed around the brass door-handle. It felt cool and solid, the exact opposite of the heated maelstrom of wild emotion that beat in her veins. She pulled the door open.

She breathed in, to the bottom of her lungs. 'I'm sorry to ruin your plans, then,' she said into the quiet of the room, 'but I'm not afraid to admit how I feel. Let me be the first to tell you that you're loved, even though it scares me. I love you, but I won't stand by and see that love wasted on some-one who lacks the courage to return it. I may never love anyone else as much as this. I can't imagine how I could. But to grow and thrive, love must be given and received equally. Be unqualified and unconditional.'

'If I asked you to stay…'

She had to swallow a sob, knowing what saying that must have cost him.

'But I have nothing to offer you…' he added.

She shook her head, weary of this. 'You don't get it, do you? I want nothing from you. I just want *you*.'

She closed the door carefully and returned, stiff-faced, to her suite, where she changed, pinned up her hair and packed her suitcase. When she went to find George to explain to him that she had to leave, she found Alex had taken him swimming, earlier than usual. She wrote him a letter, instead, and gave it to Maria, asking her to make sure someone read it to him.

Alex had evidently given instructions to Maria and Iannis about her departure. Maria was grim-faced, shaking her head and muttering in Greek, and she put her arms around Beatrice and kissed her cheek. Iannis came into the kitchen and offered to fetch her luggage.

'My instructions are to take you across to Kefalonia on the *Penelope*,' he said, gruffly, managing to sound sympathetic and disapproving at the same time.

Beatrice shook her head. 'I'd prefer to go to the ferry port, please.'

The memories she had of sharing a starlit picnic on the *Penelope* with Alex were too precious to be spoiled by the sadness of leaving.

A particular kind of silence hung over the Villa Eirini when Alex and George returned from their trip to the beach. It reached into the furthest corners of the old building and settled on his shoulders like a weighted blanket.

It was how he'd felt two years ago, when he'd arrived with a bewildered toddler, no idea how to raise him and determined not to break the habit of a lifetime and ask for help.

When George was settled in the kitchen with Maria supervising his supper he walked through the silent house towards his rooms.

There was nowhere that did not hold a memory. The window alcove where he and Beatrice had stood and he'd experienced that first, almost overwhelming need to kiss her; the door to her suite, where he hesitated but forced himself to keep moving past because going in would unravel him completely. Entering his bedroom took huge effort and then the hint of her perfume on the air stole his breath and almost his mind. He opened the windows, but found he was scanning the sweep of sea between Ithaca and Kefalonia for any sign of the *Penelope*.

At George's bedtime he read her letter to him and tried to add his own halting explanation. George's solemn blue eyes filled with tears and his bottom lip trembled. Alex struggled to comfort him, afraid that hugging him would be his undoing and yet knowing how Beatrice would hate seeing him retreat behind the remote façade he'd worked hard to banish. He reflected bitterly that he was in as much need of comfort as the four-year-old boy, only he was solely to blame for the pall of depression that hung over everyone.

He cancelled dinner and sat on the terrace cradling a tumbler of whisky, the bottle at his elbow, and acknowledged that there was no escape from Beatrice on Ithaca. Every room reminded him of her presence, of her wide smile, her soft laugh. Even more difficult were the intense, private memories, of the small sounds she made in her throat when his tongue slid against hers, or the tantalising vanilla and rose scent of her skin when he carried her from the shower to bed.

The Villa Eirini had felt like a home, with Beatrice in it. Without her it was merely a grand old house.

He wished he could forget her parting words. She'd accused him of being afraid of emotion. He thought about the avalanche of emotions he'd had to navigate when he'd learned he had a son. He'd been shocked. Guilt-ridden. But not afraid. He'd dealt with the trauma by flinging himself at the task, treating it like a business deal and project. He'd retreated to Ithaca, hired Dafni, drawn up timetables and rules. He'd been so certain he could control everything.

Love? Anger made his fist tighten around the glass. Since he'd given up hoping for it as a boy, he'd made sure that he was never going to fall into that trap again. He'd failed to protect his sister from its dangerous consequences, but he would never, ever be blinded by its false light. How could anyone ever be sure love was true?

So that he'd never be in doubt, he'd decided he'd never love anyone. That way, no one would ever love him back. You couldn't fear losing something you'd never had. George had changed that. He loved him with a ferocity that shocked him, but that was because he was his father. No one could take that away from him.

CHAPTER EIGHTEEN

THE MEET AND greet line-up snaked beneath the crystal chandeliers of the grand foyer of the sumptuous hotel, and everyone who was anyone in Greek or Italian society seemed to be in it.

Polished women in elegant designer gowns dazzled in glittering jewellery, men in sleek tuxes at their elbows.

Beatrice joined the line to the party everyone wanted to be at, wishing she was somewhere else entirely. She'd splashed out on her turquoise dress with a ruched, sequinned bodice and a floaty chiffon skirt, telling herself she'd have done the same for Enzo and Thaleia's wedding, had she been invited.

She kept her head down until she reached the elaborate doorway.

Enzo's face split into the grin she knew and loved so well. Instead of following protocol and taking her hand, he swept her into his arms, kissing her on both cheeks, then, keeping an arm around her, he circled his other arm around the waist of the dark-haired, green-eyed woman who stood beside him.

'Thaleia, look who's here!'

'Beatrice?' Thaleia's formal expression of welcome transformed into one of delight. She seized Beatrice's hands. 'Oh, we are *so* delighted that you've come.' She followed Enzo's example by kissing Beatrice warmly. Then she peered beyond her and a small frown creased her smooth forehead. 'My brother…?'

Beatrice raised her chin. 'I left Ithaca two weeks ago to return to Switzerland.' A tendril of hair curled around her face, and she tucked it behind her ear, hoping nobody would notice the tremor in her hand. 'I don't know where he is.'

'You left?' Enzo frowned. 'But you sounded so happy when we spoke.'

'Enzo, there is a line of people waiting to greet you.' Beatrice gestured behind her. 'Perhaps we can talk later, although you're going to be very busy, circulating.' She smiled, feeling her cheeks might crack from the strain.

He nodded and squeezed her shoulders. 'You're right. There'll be time to catch up later.' He turned his attention to the next couple. But Thaleia kept hold of her hands, her eyes searching her face. 'Oh, Beatrice, my brother…' She shook her head.

Beatrice pulled her hands away. 'I'm fine, really. It's just…'

She turned away, wanting to be swallowed up

in the crowd. Loud conversation buzzed around her, drowning out the music from the string quartet, which played on a stage. She grabbed a flute of champagne from the tray of a passing waiter and took three large gulps.

It had only taken seconds, but she'd seen the flash of understanding cross Thaleia's face and the sympathy that glazed her soft eyes.

Eyes that were so like Alex's that it hurt her to look at them, and the resemblance didn't end there. Her glossy hair fell in waves around her shoulders, forcing Beatrice to relive all the times she'd pushed her fingers into Alex's thick, dark locks, and how he'd groaned when she'd scraped her nails lightly across his scalp.

Thaleia's full lips were like an exaggerated form of Alex's sculpted mouth, and the sight of her elegant hands, so like her brother's, sent such a punch of painful memory to her stomach that she had to try not to double over.

This was much harder than she'd thought it would be. She felt shocked and shaky. Panic fluttered below her ribs at the realisation that Alex and George no longer had anything to do with her. And how was she going to navigate the future, when her new sister-in-law reminded her so much of the man she loved but who would never love her back.

Two weeks in her apartment in Geneva had been torture. She'd ached to hear Alex's deep voice, feel his sure, gentle caress, smell his unique scent of citrus and cedar. She'd worried that George might be unhappy. She missed the warm, dry air of Ithaca, the salty tang of the sea and the sharp sweetness of the lemon grove, which would always remind her of the first time Alex took her up the secret stairway to his rooms. And she missed knowing that every evening, when the elegant mansion was silent, she'd hear Alex's footsteps, feel his arm slide around her waist and his lips touch the sensitive spot where her neck joined her shoulder, and she'd turn into his arms, finding his mouth with hers.

She'd come to Enzo and Thaleia's glittering party in Rome because she'd promised she would. She wanted to put things right with her brother and meet his new wife. She'd mistakenly believed Alex would want the same.

When Enzo and Thaleia had greeted all their guests, they'd moved into the ballroom to mingle, but even when they were apart, Beatrice could see they were connected, always aware of where the other was in the milling crowd.

She remembered how she'd loved knowing Alex's eyes were still on her, even when she'd turned away from him, and now she felt fractured by loss and longing. Seeing Enzo and Thaleia's happiness, how they so obviously shared a deep understanding of each other, brought home to her the raw truth that she and Alex would never be together. The idea of love scared him and he'd let her go rather than dare to admit it into his life.

When she caught a glimpse of his parents, Nicholas and Helena, threading their way through the throng in her direction, she knew she had to leave. The thought of facing their speculative glances and probing questions made her stomach cramp.

Beatrice ducked behind a marble column and made her escape. At the hotel reception desk, she wrote a note of apology to Enzo and Thaleia, pleading a headache, and asked the liveried doorman to call a taxi.

Alex stood at the entrance to the ballroom and glowered over the heads of all the people to whom he really, truly didn't want to have to talk. There was only one face he was searching for, and right now he couldn't find it.

Okay, he knew he was going to have to engage with his errant little sister, now *Mrs Capelli*, and his former best friend. It was their delayed wedding party, and good manners dictated that he'd need to congratulate them.

He straightened his bow-tie and slipped a hand into the pocket of his tux.

He saw his parents first and his jaw tightened, but then he realised, with a sense of relief, that he no longer cared about their opinion. In his heart he knew his intention to be a good father to George was strong. Letting go of the burden of expectation they'd placed on him for so long felt stupidly easy.

Much more difficult was the knowledge that he had to admit he could not bear being without Beatrice.

He needed to see her. Make sure she was okay. She'd said she loved him and had accused him of being afraid to face his feelings.

He'd told her how much he prized honesty and yet he hadn't been honest with her. He had to admit to his fear of being vulnerable. He had to tell her…what? The way she made him feel felt fathomless and boundless, and that scared him. He needed order and control but did that mean navigating the rest of his life in this emptiness, without her? What if he'd hurt her and damaged what they'd shared beyond repair. He'd hidden behind his guilt about breaking his word to Enzo and his stubborn pride and refusal to acknowledge their love had stopped him from forgiving him and Thaleia for their marriage. He'd driven away the one person who loved him, not for his wealth, success or ancient lineage, but unconditionally for himself, and in letting her go, George had had someone who loved him torn from his life for a second time.

Then he saw Thaleia. She looked radiant in a deep red silk dress, her luxuriant hair tumbling over her shoulders. Her smile softened and widened as the man next to her slid his arm around her slim waist. His stomach clenched at the way their eyes connected with each other, at the understanding and emotion that flowed between them, and finally he knew with absolute certainty what he had to say to Beatrice.

Once, he'd joked that the only thing that frightened him was the idea of love and marriage. Now he knew how wrong he'd been. What terrified him now was that he might have lost Beatrice forever.

Enzo. Alex's hands closed into fists.

As if his heated glare had burned them, Enzo and Thaleia turned. He saw their momentary confusion quickly erased and then they started towards him.

'Alex.' Thaleia slipped her arms around his shoulders and kissed him. 'We thought you weren't coming.'

'I wasn't. But…' His eyes strayed to the crowd behind them, searching for Beatrice.

'*Dion.*' His attention snapped back, caught by the sound of his old college nickname. 'We're pleased to see you.' Alex made a conscious effort to focus on Thaleia and Enzo. 'Although,' Enzo continued, softly, 'you don't look that pleased to see us.'

'My plans changed,' he said, stiffly, allowing Enzo to shake his hand. 'Congratulations.'

Enzo nodded. 'Thank you. But should we assume it's not really us you've come to see?'

Alex ran an agitated hand through his hair. His jaw ached with tension. When George had asked, in a small voice, why Beatrice had gone, like his mummy, his determination had finally cracked and desperation to see her had overwhelmed him. His journey from Ithaca had been plagued by delays. Even though he'd told George he was going to find her, he had thrown a wobbly when he'd said he was leaving him with Dafni, who'd answered his plea and returned to Ithaca for a few days. He'd had to use the ferry because Iannis was varnishing the *Penelope*'s deck, and his jet had been held on the runway by a summer storm. He'd changed in the cabin after they'd landed in Rome, and the car he'd booked had brought him directly to this hotel, late and irritable.

Beatrice would be at this party and once the idea of coming to find her had taken hold he couldn't shake it. He couldn't have remained on Ithaca another day. He had to talk to her, if she would talk to him.

When Thaleia fixed her steady eyes on his face he knew he was in deep trouble. Since when had the boot been on her foot and not on his? He'd lost track of her—of everyone—when George had arrived in his life. Things had changed, moved on. She was no longer the little sister he'd spent his life protecting from the cold and unloving relationship of his parents. She was a successful businesswoman and married to one of the richest men he knew.

His best friend, who'd promised never to lay a finger on her. He turned his attention back to him.

'You broke your promise, Enzo.'

Enzo's eyes narrowed. 'And can you tell me, hand on your heart, that you did not?'

His scrutiny made Alex pause. 'Yes,' said Thaleia quietly. 'Can you, Alex?'

'What has she told you?'

Enzo and Thaleia exchanged glances.

'She didn't need to tell us anything, Dion. It was obvious. But you've hurt her, and that's much, much worse than breaking the vow we made so long ago when we were young and reckless. Yes, I broke it first. I would have talked to you, if you'd been available to talk, but nothing you said would have stopped us from being together. From marrying. My love for her is…simply boundless.' He kissed Thaleia's cheek.

'If you've lost her, you're an idiot, big bro.' Thaleia patted his arm. 'One day, if you stop trying to prove how independent you are, how impervious to your feelings, how strong your control, you might realise that. I just hope it's not too late.'

Alex closed his eyes for a moment, exhaustion tugging at the edges of his consciousness. He was tired of being angry, of holding himself together, of telling himself he was better off alone. He needed to hear her soft voice, smell the notes of her perfume, feel her palm on his jaw as she leaned in to kiss him. He needed to feel whole again.

'Just tell me if she's here,' he bit out.

'It's not easy to find someone in this crowd, but she seems to have vanished.' Thaleia frowned. 'I'll ask at reception if anyone has seen her.'

A minute later she returned, heels tapping quickly across the marble floor, a single sheet of paper clutched in her fingers.

She put a hand on Alex's arm and shook her head. 'She's gone.'

CHAPTER NINETEEN

When would her shattered heart feel whole again? Perhaps never, because a piece of it would remain forever on the fabled Island of Ithaca, where a big man and a small boy would continue their lives, without her.

Since the accident, which she'd so randomly survived, she'd tried to do everything right. Her eight-year-old self had questioned whether she'd been to blame for what had happened. Had she done something terrible and was being paid back by the universe? She had been an adult before she recognised that she suffered from survivor's guilt.

She'd been painfully, meticulously good. She'd obeyed all the rules, believing compliance would keep her world manageable and safe. Then she'd stepped out of that safety zone, when Enzo had hurt her, and gone to Ithaca, daring to think she could deceive Alex. Was this heartbreak her punishment?

She'd still believed, as the attraction between her and Alex had spiralled, that she could manage it. At the end of the summer she would leave, taking with her a perfect set of memories, safely hidden, never to be shared. Ithaca would forever remain her sacred place, where the outside world would never intrude.

The universe had a different idea. If she needed proof of how badly wrong she'd got things, it was here, in the way the memories of Alex spilled everywhere, running like quicksilver through her life, impossible to contain or compartmentalise. They invaded every corner. Everything she wore, ate or heard echoed of him. They'd been so at one, so perfectly attuned, that nothing could separate her from him now. Every word, look or touch between them had spoken volumes and those conversations, actual or silent, bound her to him in a never-ending circle of memory.

Somehow, she had to break it, to resume her old life, but in a completely altered shape. In the heat of what had happened between them, her love for him had been forged, as pure and strong as steel.

After the party she'd intended to stay in Rome, to spend time with Enzo and Thaleia, but she couldn't face their questions or sympathy, or even the possible 'I told you so' which Enzo might imply. Mostly, she couldn't face getting to know Thaleia better. Not yet, because everything about her would be a painful reminder of Alex.

She returned to her hotel, packed and changed her flight to the following morning.

By the time she'd walked through the arrivals hall at Geneva airport she knew she couldn't return to her apartment. It was no longer a place of refuge. In the previous two weeks it had felt like a prison where she'd been trapped with her memories and the consequences of her actions.

Instead, she bought a train ticket for Lauterbrunnen. It was a long journey, involving changing trains three times, but there was no hurry. She'd reach her destination in the late afternoon and there, in the chalet in the Alps, which had belonged to their parents and which Enzo had spent an untold amount of money modernising and renovating, she'd find the solitary peace she needed.

The final leg of her journey was on the cog railway, which clanked up the steep slopes en route to the heights and glamour of the Jungfraujoch. It was almost four o'clock in the afternoon by the time the train stopped, disgorging hikers who planned to take the walking trail back down to the valley. Beatrice lagged behind them, then looked up to the spectacular chalet, perched high above her. The wide windows reflected the snow-capped mountains that encircled the valley and the grasses and flowers of the alpine meadow in which it stood rippled in the breeze.

She closed her eyes against the dazzle of the afternoon sun and breathed in the crisp mountain air. The heat of Ithaca, the beloved feeling of Alex's arms wrapping around her, his mouth finding its way from her lips, down the side of her neck to the hollow at her throat, felt desperately far away.

She shouldered her holdall and began to climb up the narrow track.

Every international flight he'd taken, crossing multiple time zones, to seal a deal or solve a problem had been simple, compared with this.

He couldn't remember when he'd last slept. Except he could. It was the last night he and Beatrice had spent together. After his dash to Rome, he'd paced the floor of his hotel suite, waiting for the moment he could leave for the airport and have his pilot fly him to Geneva.

Enzo and Thaleia had not known where Beatrice was staying. The best Enzo could offer had been her address in Geneva.

Then somewhere over the Italian Alps, Enzo had called him. He'd been in touch with the concierge desk of her apartment—the guy certainly took his role of Big Brother seriously—and learned that Beatrice had left two days ago and not yet returned.

'But,' Enzo had said, 'there is one other option. Do you remember the time we went skiing on the Jungfrau and stayed in my family chalet? She might…'

Alex had cut the call and asked his pilot if he could get permission from air traffic control to divert to Bern. It was closer to Lauterbrunnen than Geneva. He called ahead to hire a car.

This was the end of the trail and she wasn't here, either. He lowered himself to the ground, the adrenalin that had kept him going since he'd left Ithaca draining away, leaving him exhausted and shaky.

He could hear the clunking of the cog railway as it climbed towards the station, the distant clank of cow-bells ringing in the high pastures. The train stopped, a group of hikers leaving it and heading towards the trailhead, then it creaked away, across the shoulder of the mountain and out of sight, with only the solitary figure of a young woman left on the path below. The sun struck copper sparks from her chestnut hair, which drifted around her shoulders, and she lifted her bag and began to walk.

His tired brain tried to do the maths. Was it possible that he'd arrived here before Beatrice?

To leap up and plunge down the slope would be tempting fate. What if his eyes were playing tricks on him and it was someone else entirely? He unfolded himself and stood, afraid of disappointment, holding himself still by sheer force of will, convinced that if he averted his eyes even for a split second, she'd disappear like a wisp of mist.

Then she raised a hand and tucked a lock of hair behind her ear in a gesture so achingly familiar that it stole his breath.

Ignoring the safety of the winding track, he struck out in a direct line downhill towards her, running where the terrain allowed it, and swearing softly when the steep slope slowed him down.

He saw her stop and drop her bag. He leapt down the last few feet of the slope and landed in front of her. He wanted to seize her and hold on to her and never release her from his arms again. But she stepped back and his heart sank. Her eyes filled with confusion and he remembered, sharply, the hurt in them when she'd walked away from him.

What if the hurt had been too deep? What would he ever do if she'd decided she never wanted to see him again?

'Beatrice.'

'What are you doing here?' She looked up at him, frowning, her teeth catching her bottom lip.

'I can't be without you for another day.' The relief at seeing her was all-consuming. His breath rasped in his throat and then his voice dropped. 'When you left you took a part of me with you, and I need you to bring it back. Please. Because otherwise I…'

She hesitated for several agonising heartbeats. Then she stepped forwards and wrapped her arms around him, pressing her face into his shoulder.

'Oh, Alex…'

'Shh.' Her hair was as silky as he remembered under his hand.

He closed his eyes, a sense of peace, of wholeness and completeness surging through him as he adjusted his hold on her, vowing to himself that he would do anything to keep her there, to never again have to feel that ripped-out emptiness her absence had left in him. He rested his cheek on her warm hair and risked releasing an arm from around her back so that he could stroke his fingers across her cheek.

She nodded, rubbing against his crumpled and travel-worn shirt. 'I left a part of my heart with you, too, and it can never mend if I don't have all the pieces. I'm afraid I'll be broken forever, without you.'

His fingertips drew small circles between her shoulder blades. 'Do you remember me telling you never to be afraid of me?'

'Yes, I do. But I'm afraid of my feelings for you. They feel so dangerous.'

'I'm afraid, too.' He kissed the top of her head. 'I'm afraid that if I let myself love you I might lose you and that terrifies me, but the thought of living without you terrifies me more. So I want to ask you…'

'Are you saying you might try to love me?'

'No, I'm saying I *do* love you.' He tightened his hold on her. 'I've never loved anyone else. I *could* never love anyone else. You ground me, and yet in your arms I can fly free, knowing I'm safe, knowing I'm enough for you. Hearing you say you loved me was…' He swallowed. 'Was so wonderful it *hurt*. I knew at that moment that I loved you, too, but I refused to admit it. I'd spent my life denying the very existence of love, but I think I've always been searching for it. With you I know I've found it. So, if you meant it, if you still mean it…if you can forgive me for hurting you…'

She pulled his mouth down to hers. Her lips parted and his tongue slipped into her warm sweetness. He stroked trembling fingers over her face, desperate to reassure himself that he remembered every detail.

'I'm sorry, Alex.' She breathed the words against his mouth, and he stilled, dreading what she might say.

'Beatrice. Please don't…'

'I'm sorry I accused you of being afraid.'

'But I *was* afraid to admit that I loved you.' He exhaled. 'I was arrogant and stubborn. I thought I could forget you. But I don't want to.'

'You were afraid, but you've had the courage to be humble and face your fear. And yes, I meant what I said.' Her voice caught and she swallowed. 'I love you, with my whole heart and soul and being.'

The view of the towering mountains framed in the wide window faded into insignificance next to the sight of Alex lying next to her. Toned muscle rippled beneath bronzed skin, his untidy dark hair a startling contrast against the white bedlinen.

Beatrice propped her head in her hand and trailed her fingers over his chest, smiling as his breath caught. His eyes fluttered open, and a smile ghosted across his lips.

'There's no hope of catching up on all the sleep I've lost over you.'

'Shall I leave you alone?'

'Don't you dare.' He pulled her down so that he could kiss her mouth.

'Will you tell me how you found me? And how is George?'

He sat up against the pillows and drew her head down to his chest.

'I might have to take a break in between answering your questions.'

'Have I worn you out?'

'I meant I might have to take a break from questions to make love to you again.'

Her skin shivered as he trailed a finger over her shoulder. 'Promise?'

'Promise. George misses you. We need you to come back. Please.'

'I'm sorry. It's hard for him to understand.'

'His world will make sense when he sees you again, as mine does.'

She turned her head a little, pressing her mouth to his breastbone, loving how his breathing stuttered.

'I suggested to Enzo that he should come up with some creative ideas about where you might be, and quickly.'

'You saw Enzo?'

'I went to the party, but you'd left.'

She twisted her head to look up at him. 'I went…and then I met Thaleia and she's so like you. I…couldn't stay.'

'Enzo said you hadn't been back to your apartment in Geneva and this place was his only other suggestion. I once came skiing here with him. I flew to Bern and hired a car. When you weren't here…' His fingers stilled in her hair and his breath hissed. 'I don't think I've ever felt more alone. And then when I saw you, I was suddenly afraid that you wouldn't want to see me.'

Beatrice raised her head. 'Seeing you was like…it was like becoming weightless…'

He pulled her fiercely against him. 'Will you marry me, Beatrice? Please be my wife, and George's mother.' He kissed her and kissed her, his hands cupping her face, sliding into her hair, angling her head for better access. 'You bring such joy. We can stay in Geneva, if you want—I can work from anywhere.' Beatrice smiled under his mouth, pushing gently at his shoulders. 'George can go to your school and we can spend the holidays on Ithaca…' He pulled back a little, his eyes dark and questioning.

Beatrice's tried to speak past the emotion clogging her throat. She swallowed, wiping away tears with the back of her hand, and tried again. 'You'd do that for me?'

'I'd do anything in the world for you. Please tell me…'

She placed a finger over his lips. 'Yes, oh, Alex, yes,' she whispered.

EPILOGUE

IANNIS BROUGHT THE *Penelope* alongside the jetty. He handed a coil of rope to George, then he leapt ashore and caught the line that George threw to him.

George turned towards Beatrice and Alex, a grin splitting his face. 'I did it!' He was a little taller than he'd been just under a year ago and a lot more confident.

Alex's arm tightened around Beatrice's shoulders, pulling her closer to his side. He turned his head to kiss her temple. The softness of her skin still surprised him whenever his lips touched her, which, he admitted, was multiple times a day.

He'd never tire of kissing her, or of having her close, or of holding her in his arms all night.

He held out his free arm to George. 'Well done. Iannis will make a captain of you before long. Come here.'

George high-fived him. 'Iannis says I can help tie the ropes, as soon as it's safe to jump onto the jetty.'

It was late afternoon, and they'd left Geneva that morning on the first day of the holidays. George had been fizzing with excitement at the prospect of spending the summer on Ithaca, and of the party they were going to have. Friends were coming from all over the world to celebrate their marriage.

Beatrice's cheek rested on his shoulder, and he glanced down at her. 'Tired?'

'A little. But excited to be here, and for three months. Bliss!' She stood, keeping hold of his hand as the launch rose and fell on the slight swell. 'I love my job, and all my pupils, but…' She sighed, turning her face up to the sun. 'Nothing compares with the magic of Ithaca.'

He smiled, squeezing her hand. 'Mm. It used to be my favourite place.'

'*Used* to be?'

'My new favourite place is wherever you are. You make everywhere magical.'

George, watched by Iannis, was winding a rope around a bollard with single-minded attention. Alex's heart swelled with love and pride. George had grown from the traumatised, silent child he'd first brought to Ithaca into this independent little boy. He'd loved his first year at the school in Geneva where Beatrice taught. She'd worked her magic on him, as she did on everyone. It was one of the million things, and counting, he loved about her.

'We've got the Villa Eirini to ourselves for two

whole days, before wedding guests start arriving.' His eyes narrowed as he studied Beatrice. She looked a little pale, but it had been a busy term and a long day. Naturally, she was tired. 'You'll have time to rest.'

He lifted her hand to kiss her palm and the diamond ring on her finger sparkled. She smiled. 'It'll be especially exciting to see Enzo and Thaleia.'

'Mm. I know Thaleia must be hot and uncomfortable, but I hope their baby waits until after our wedding before arriving.'

Alex followed her across the gangplank Iannis had put in place, his hand on the small of her back, and then they walked, his arm around her shoulders, to where the Jeep waited in the shade.

Beatrice slid her arm around his waist. 'Alex?'

'What is it, my love? You sound anxious.'

'Just pre-wedding nerves.'

'Everything is in place. All you have to do is turn up looking beautiful, which you do, effortlessly, every day, anyway.'

'The thing is, I'm afraid my dress might not fit.'

'Why?'

She took his hand and rested his palm on her abdomen. 'Because…'

Alex went completely still, disbelief and then joy flooding through him. He stared down into her soft, grey eyes. 'Are you sure? When? Oh, sweetheart…'

He enfolded her in his arms, feeling her heart beating in time with his, too full of emotion for words.

'Daddy!'

George ran over to them, and Alex pulled him into their embrace, holding the two people he loved most in the world with a fierceness he found difficult to comprehend.

'We're going to be a complete family,' he whispered. 'The Villa Eirini will be a proper home again. It's more than I ever believed possible. I love you both so, so much.'

'I said once before that I could never love anyone more than I love you.' He felt the strength of Beatrice's love flowing through him and his son. 'To be your wife, and the mother of George and our baby, feels—almost too much for my heart.'

George twisted out from under his arm and went back to help Iannis.

'My love for you and George would feel overwhelming, and scary, but you've given me the courage to be vulnerable. I know my heart is safe with you, and I'll prove to you every day that yours is safe with me.'

He cupped her cheek in his palm and tipped her head back, brushing his mouth across her lips. 'And this is just one of the ways I'll show you.'

* * * * *

If you missed the previous story in the
A Pact Between Tycoons duet, then check out

The Trouble with Italian Millionaires
by Karin Baine

And if you enjoyed this story, check out these
other great reads from Suzanne Merchant

Conveniently Engaged to a Princess
Best Man's Second Chance
Cinderella's Adventure with the CEO

All available now!